HARRY FLAMMABLE

a novel

Frank O'Keeffe

DUNDURN
TORONTO

Editor: Jennifer McKnight
Design: Courtney Horner
Printer: Webcom

Library and Archives Canada Cataloguing in Publication

O'Keeffe, Frank
    Harry Flammable / Frank O'Keeffe.

Issued also in electronic formats.
ISBN 978-1-4597-0454-1

    I. Title.

PS8579.K44H37 2013   jC813'.54   C2012-903218-2

1   2   3   4   5   17   16   15   14   13

We acknowledge the support of the **Canada Council for the Arts** and the **Ontario Arts Council** for our publishing program. We also acknowledge the financial support of the **Government of Canada** through the **Canada Book Fund** and **Livres Canada Books**, and the **Government of Ontario** through the **Ontario Book Publishing Tax Credit** and the **Ontario Media Development Corporation**.

Printed and bound in Canada.

Visit us at
Dundurn.com
Definingcanada.ca
@dundurnpress
Facebook.com/dundurnpress

Dundurn
3 Church Street, Suite 500
Toronto, Ontario, Canada
M5E 1M2

Gazelle Book Services Limited
White Cross Mills
High Town, Lancaster, England
LA1 4XS

Dundurn
2250 Military Road
Tonawanda, NY
U.S.A. 14150

For my wife Patricia who knows who she is, with my love always
For Kevin who toiled in many a hotel kitchen
For Iván Guevara our Cuban son
and
In memory of Martyn Godfrey

"Okay, Harry. Tell me again. Where were you when the equipment shed burned down?"

Mr. Shamberg slowly put his large hands together like he was going to pray, rested his chin on the tips of his fingers, closed his eyes, and waited.

I took a deep breath and accidentally swallowed my gum. *Not much for a condemned man's last meal*, I thought. Mr. Shamberg, my judge and executioner, still had his eyes closed. His huge body filled the space behind his tiny desk and his massive head blocked most of my view of the poster that hung on the wall behind him. Despite the trouble I was in, I couldn't help smiling at the way Mr. Shamberg's frizzy tufts of red hair blended with those of the orangutan on the poster. That was all I could see of the orangutan, but I knew it was hanging from a branch of a tree by one arm, and I knew the poster's caption by heart — "Hang in There Baby!"

Maybe Mr. Shamberg had fallen asleep. No such luck. One big, hairy red eyebrow moved upward and I quickly wiped the smile off my face. The eye opened and regarded me. "Well, Harry, where were you?"

"I was at home in bed like I said. Honest."

Mr. Shamberg's other eye popped open. Then he started that tuneless whistling that he always does when he thinks someone is lying. It's the only time he ever whistles and he's hopeless at it. He thinks he's whistling some real old song called "They Wouldn't Believe Me." I know that's supposed to be the song he's trying to whistle. He told us in class one day because Barbara Law had given him a really dumb excuse for not getting some assignment done on time. He'd started whistling the tune and asked Barbara if she knew the name of it. She guessed it might be "Your Cheatin' Heart." It could have been anything. Mr. Shamberg's whistling is so bad, it's more like a boiling kettle's whistling than anything else. We'd all started guessing the name of the tune then, just to waste time, and Mr. Shamberg finally had to tell us.

"Home in bed, Harry? Really? And I suppose your whole family will swear to that?"

"I guess so. It's true."

"Then how do you account for this?" He reached down behind his desk and picked up something black from the floor. I stared at it. The way Mr. Shamberg held it between his thumb and forefinger, I thought it must be something disgusting. He let it drop onto the edge of his desk in front of me and a small cloud of black dust rose into the air. It looked like a dead cat.

"But I don't own a cat," I leaned away from the thing. It smelled bad.

"Cat?" Mr. Shamberg looked puzzled. "Don't you mean cap, Harry?" He reached out and gingerly picked up the blackened lump again, turned it slowly and then let it fall back onto the desk. Another puff of black dust drifted upwards.

Although it was slightly melted, I could still recognize the Second World War silver metal badge of the Luftwaffe, the German Airforce. I was the only kid in the school who had one. The black smelly thing on the desk was the remains of my black leather and cloth Dutch fisherman's cap. I'd found the cap in the sporting goods catalogue a year ago and sent away for it, and I'd bought the badge in a store that sold war memorabilia. The store owner told me at the time that the badge was a hard to find item and it had cost me twenty bucks. I'd worn that cap with its badge every day. It was my trademark.

"Your cap was found in the remains of the shed, along with, I might add," here Mr. Shamberg took a deep breath, "my brand new, just paid for, thousand dollar mountain bike."

I gulped. The shed was just an old shack. As far as I knew it was used to store a few track and field items like the poles for the high jump, a bunch of traffic cones for marking the field boundaries, and the old machine the school used to paint the white lines on the grass.

"So, Harry. Why did you do it?"

"I didn't."

"This is your cap. It was found in what's left of the shed. You might as well tell me all about it."

I sighed. Mr. Shamberg wasn't a bad guy. He taught us a course called Life Skills, was in charge of the work experience program, and was also the school counsellor. It was his job as school counsellor at Crestwood High that had landed him the problem of sorting out who started the fire, and, now that his mountain bike had been destroyed, he had a special reason to find out who did it. I knew he was never going to believe me. I had been at home in bed, but with the remains of my cap found in the smouldering ruins, I was a dead duck. It was useless to claim I'd been framed.

The trouble is my reputation. My real name is Harry Flanagan but nearly everyone called me either "Harry Flammable" or "Highly Flammable." The younger kids in school think my real name is "Harry Flame-Again" because they get names wrong sometimes.

I guess you could say I earned my reputation, but it wasn't always my fault. I just got blamed or suspected whenever a fire broke out. Just like now, with the shed.

I'd started working on my reputation way back in second grade. Then, I'd wanted to be a movie actor or at least a stunt-man. I still do. I'd seen a guy in the movies riding a motorcycle through a flaming wall and it looked really neat. I thought I'd try it. I didn't have a motorcycle, but I did have a bicycle.

With the motorcycle, they get a big sheet of wood, put a ramp in front of it, pour gas or something on the wood, light it, and when it's really blazing well, the guy on the motorcycle races up the ramp and bursts through the flaming wall. I couldn't find a big enough sheet of wood but Leonard Wooleys' parents had just bought a new fridge and the cardboard box that the fridge came in was in their backyard. Leonard's mom said we could have the box.

We found a plank and a couple of bricks to make a ramp, and took the box to a piece of rough land a few blocks from our place. There are new houses there now, but then it was an open, grassy spot with a few trees. We used it as our private playground, building forts and playing war. Matthew Beagle got a book of matches and siphoned a little bit of gasoline from his dad's lawnmower into a pop bottle. All the way to the vacant lot he kept spitting to get the taste of the gasoline out of his mouth, and he kept saying he wasn't going to light the match because he might blow up.

We got everything set up. Leonard splashed the gas onto the fridge box and tried to light it, but the matches kept going out.

We had only one match left when I got the idea of lighting some dry grass first and then using it to light the box. It worked. There was a loud *whomp*. Matthew was sure he was blowing up and dove for cover as flames shot up all over the box. I raced back to where I'd left my bike and got ready. Leonard had a piece of red rag tied on a stick to give me the signal to go. Matthew came out from behind a tree to watch when he realized he was still okay.

Leonard gave me the signal and I raced towards the box. I know now the motorcycle guys who do this stunt wait until the wood is almost burned through and they go a lot faster than a bicycle. The fridge box was burning fiercely but, unlike a flat sheet of wood, it had four burning sides and a big space in the middle.

I pedalled like mad at the flaming box, aiming at the foot of the ramp. Close to the plank, my front wheel skidded on some loose sand and my wheel knocked the plank off the bricks. I was going sideways when I hit the box.

My bike stopped but I didn't. I flew off it through the front wall of the box and landed in a heap inside it. Smoke filled my nose and eyes and I felt the heat from the flames. I smelled the stench of burning hair as I scrambled to my feet. I plunged through the other side of the box with a piece of it dangling and blazing around my neck. I rolled on the ground and beat at my chest where my t-shirt felt hot. When I could see, I found a large black hole in my shirt.

Leonard had managed to drag my bike from under the collapsed box. He was pointing at my head and laughing.

The top of my hair was all crispy, and bits flaked off like dust when I touched it. Under my chin the skin was smarting where the cardboard had burned me. Matthew pointed out that my eyebrows were gone too.

But that wasn't all. The dry grass that covered the piece of land had caught fire and a breeze had sprung up, fanning the flames. We did our best to beat the flames out with our jackets, but it was hopeless. The fire was out of control and we had to retreat. We retreated even further when we heard the sound of sirens and a fire truck raced up the street.

When we went back later we found that our tree fort was a blackened ruin. Of course the word got out. I couldn't hide my singed hair and eyebrows and Mom took me to the doctor to have the burn on my neck treated. A fireman came to the school a few days later to give us a talk about the danger of fires and, during his whole talk, all the kids stared at me. Then they nicknamed me "the Fireman."

That was the beginning. Other fires broke out from time to time, and, even if I was nowhere near when they happened, there were always whispers. Okay, I admit it. It was me in seventh grade who turned on the Bunsen burner in the science lab and stood it in the window in the sun so you couldn't see the flame. It made a really great roaring noise and the flame was invisible. But how was I to know we were going to have a substitute teacher that day and he was partially deaf? It wasn't my fault he decided to sit on the lab counter right in front of the Bunsen burner and caught the back of his sweater on fire.

By that time I was known as Harry Flammable and I think it was around then that some kid threw a cigarette butt into a garbage can in Ms. Maltin's French class. We were ten minutes into the period when flames started shooting out of the can. Ms. Maltin and some of the kids got the fire out and we got back to the lesson, but when Ms. Maltin was walking past my desk, the book I was reading at the time happened to fall out of my desk, right at her feet. It was *Firestarter* by Stephen King. It was pure coincidence — I happen to like Stephen King. But as Ms. Maltin put the book back on my desk, I knew what she was thinking.

"Well, Harry. I'd say you don't have a leg to stand on." Mr. Shamberg was still waiting for an explanation.

It was useless to tell him that yesterday, just after school,

Joe Straka had grabbed my cap off my head and taken off with it. I'd chased him, but he ran around the side of the school and when I got there, he'd disappeared.

I shrugged. "I didn't do it," I repeated.

Mr. Shamberg started whistling his version of "They Wouldn't Believe Me" again.

Out of the corner of my eye I noticed a thin column of smoke rising from the remains of my cap. Mr. Shamberg didn't notice. He was whistling away and staring at the ceiling. When he'd picked up my cap and twirled it around on his desk, there must have been a small ember still smoldering. He'd given it just enough oxygen to get it started again.

I was about to say something when Mr. Shamberg stopped whistling.

"Okay Harry. I've wasted enough time on this. You've been caught red-handed, so to speak. You might even say, 'If the cap fits, wear it.'" He chuckled at his little joke. "And in this case it certainly does. Now what I suggest …"

"But Mr. Shamberg, my cap …"

"Just let me finish. What I suggest is you …"

"But Mr. Shamberg, my cap is on fire!"

It wasn't just my cap anymore. Mr. Shamberg had dropped my cap right beside a pile of papers on his desk and, even as I spoke, a tongue of flame shot up.

"How did you do that?" Mr. Shamberg hollered.

He still sat there, not doing anything as the flame spread and began to eat a hole through the pile of papers.

I had to do something. I slapped my hand down on top of the papers and my smouldering cap. All that achieved was to scatter little black lumps of the black soot of my cap across Mr. Shamberg's desk where they glowed and pulsed, like they were about to burst into flames and start miniature fires all over his desk.

By now the papers were nearly a blackened curling pile, and still Mr. Shamberg only stared. I looked around desperately. There wasn't any jug of water handy but I spotted Mr. Shamberg's huge Thermos on a shelf beside his desk. I knew it was usually filled with coffee. That would have to do. I grabbed it, quickly unscrewed the lid and emptied the contents onto the desk. *That's weird*, I thought. *The coffee turned pink.* Then I realized that today Mr. Shamberg had decided not to bring coffee. It was tomato alphabet soup.

He came out of his trance. "Those were the midterm exams for this semester," he screamed. "Go. Just go. I'll talk to you later."

I put the Thermos down quickly on the only space on his desk that wasn't swimming in the pink slop of the soup and headed out the door.

As I made it to the hall, I thought I heard Mr. Shamberg mutter "No wonder they call him Harry *Flammable*." Like I said, I have this reputation.

But my biggest worry right then wasn't just my reputation. It was Mr. Shamberg. He held my fate in his hands. I'd just poured alphabet soup all over his desk, ruined some exams, was the only suspect in destroying the shed, not to mention his mountain bike, and tomorrow was the day he was going to tell us where we were going to be placed in the program.

I'd been anxiously waiting for that day to arrive and I knew I'd made a good case to get the job, any job, as long as it was part of the crew at Pocket Money Pictures. A week ago my chances of getting taken on by the film company, who were about to film some epic near Summervale, had looked good. Mr. Shamberg had said that, even though the competition would be tough, he'd put in a good word for me. After today, I don't think *good* would be the exact word that would spring to his lips when he mentioned my name.

2

I WAS ALREADY LATE for math class and Ms. Havershaw gave me a baleful look as I hurried to my desk.

I opened my math text and tried to concentrate on what Ms. Havershaw was saying as she wrote something on the chalkboard, but my eyes drifted to Celia Spendlove. She sat in the front row near the door and, from where I sat, three seats back on the other side of the room, I could see her clearly. I sat there admiring her sleek, dark hair, her lovely complexion, and her extraordinary long, dark eyelashes. I loved the way they rested on her cheek when she looked down at her textbook. From where I sat I could only see the one over her right eye, but I knew its twin was equally beautiful.

She'd come into our class just two weeks ago, and I'd been wondering ever since what my chances were of getting a date with her.

A few seconds later, they hit zero. It was Ralph that did it. Ms. Havershaw had just finished explaining something about some equation and told us to try the ones on page 168, when he crawled up under Celia Spendlove's skirt. It wasn't really his fault. He was only trying to stay warm. One minute he was in the shoebox on the shelf under my desk and the next thing I knew he was giving Celia Spendlove hysterics.

She gave a piercing scream and leaped to her feet, clutching her skirt just above her right knee.

I guessed right away what had happened, but I checked quickly to make sure. The lid was off the shoebox and it was empty. I ran to the front of the class where Celia stood, flapping at herself and screaming.

The rest of the class had frozen. Celia's screams were ear-piercing and Ms. Havershaw stood staring at her like she was wondering if she was going to have to deal with one of those drug-crazed teenagers she'd heard so much about.

I reached Celia and had to kneel to retrieve Ralph, my pet iguana. Celia had blocked his further advances by clamping her hands against her skirt. She didn't resist when I reached above her knee to untangle Ralph from her pantyhose.

Ms. Havershaw gasped when she saw me holding Ralph. "Get that creature out of here!" she screeched and gave a shudder. "Take it out of here at once!"

I ran to my desk and grabbed Ralph's shoebox from the shelf as the class burst into laughter. Ralph lashed his tail in anger as I stuffed him into the box and beat a hasty retreat. I put the box in my locker and returned to class. There were a few snickers from the class as I entered and as I passed Celia's desk, I whispered a quick "sorry." She was blushing furiously and Ms. Havershaw gave me a frosty look.

I cursed Ralph but it was really my own fault. I'd brought Ralph to school, intending to make a big impression by letting him ride on my shoulder at lunch time. I thought he would be a sort of conversation piece and Celia would be impressed. Some conversation piece! The class probably wouldn't stop talking about it for months.

Celia obviously disliked lizards and now, no doubt, anyone who had anything to do with them. Me.

If the classroom hadn't been so cold maybe Ralph would have stayed where he was. Ms. Havershaw believed in keeping the room like an icebox, to keep us awake. Most of us brought along an extra sweater if we remembered to check our timetables.

My chances of getting a date with Celia got even slimmer that afternoon. She kept giving me these dirty looks and I thought it was because of Ralph. I found out later some jerk had passed her a note signed with my initials that read, "Celia, can I feel ya?" If Celia's looks could kill, I'd be dead. I vowed to kill that guy if I found out who it was. It was a lousy trick.

I was getting my stuff from my locker next morning when the P.A. boomed. "If Harry Flanagan is in the school, would he please go to Mr. Shamberg's office immediately."

I groaned. I was probably in for another grilling about the fire.

"Sit down, Harry," Mr. Shamberg said as I entered. "But don't touch anything," he added hurriedly. As I sat I noticed the chair was as far away from his desk as it could possibly be.

"Okay, Harry." Mr. Shamberg almost smiled. He seemed to be in a much better mood than yesterday. "I called you in for two reasons. First, Joe Straka dropped by my office after school and told me he'd thrown your hat onto the roof of the shed. Apparently word got around your hat was found in the fire. That doesn't let you entirely off the hook. Your fame is only exceeded by your reputation, or whatever that saying is. But it does seem to explain why your hat was there in the first place.

It also appears the school insurance will look after replacing my bike. However, I want you to know that if you had anything to do with the fire it would be best to admit it. Everyone in the school is under suspicion." Mr. Shamberg paused.

"I don't know anything about it, honest."

"Okay, Harry. We'll leave it at that for now. The other reason I called you in is because today, as you know, is the day I'm going to announce the work experience job placements. I'll be doing this in class later, but I thought that, in view of our little confrontation yesterday, you might feel where you were placed would be affected. That I might be biased against you or something. I want you to know, as promised, I made a strong recommendation to Pocket Money Pictures on your behalf. I told them how keen you were."

My heart sank. I knew what was coming.

"However," Mr. Shamberg went on, "Pocket Money Pictures indicated they preferred a girl for the job. In fact, they insisted on it. I'm afraid I had to place the other leading candidate in that position."

"Who was that?" I blurted.

"Mmm … that new girl …" Mr. Shamberg searched on his desk for something, then flipped over a sheet of paper. "Here it is. Celia Spendlove. But it's not all bad news. I managed to get you one of the prime placements elsewhere."

Elsewhere. What did he mean, elsewhere? Some welding shop, some warehouse loading trucks, a supermarket bagging groceries? The only place prime for me was Pocket Money Pictures. It was going to be my first step, getting my foot in the door, to become a famous director. I didn't care what job they gave me. Just making the coffee would have been good enough, and I'd have done it for nothing. Some places paid minimum wages but others didn't. They just gave you experience. And it was the experience I wanted.

"This one pays fifty cents an hour over the minimum wage. I know you're disappointed about the film company but The Ritz Hotel is a really classy place to work. Just do me a favour. Don't burn it down, okay?"

"The Ritz? Doing what?"

"Well you know, causing accidents like yesterday with your cap," he joked. "Oh, you mean what's the job. It's working under Chef Antonio in the kitchen. He's famous. You'll learn a lot. You'll be shown how to do all sorts of exciting things."

"You mean like peeling potatoes, making Jell-O?"

"No, not necessarily. It's the best job I have. Some students would give their eye teeth to get it. I just wanted you to know it's the best I could get you and I wanted you to understand there are no hard feelings about what happened yesterday. I tried my best to get you placed with Pocket Money Pictures. But it just wasn't to be. I wanted to tell you before I have to announce it in class later."

"Thanks, Mr. Shamberg," I mumbled. I rose to leave.

"Oh, Harry. Before you go to The Ritz, you might want to get a haircut."

A haircut? My hair, which was dark, wasn't that long, just over my collar. I thought it gave me the perfect film director's look. Cut my hair? No way. Maybe I'd just tell Mr. Shamberg I wanted something else. Maybe some kids would give their eye teeth for The Ritz job like Mr. Shamberg said, but what's a few teeth compared to cutting your hair? My hair! Maybe bagging groceries wouldn't be so bad.

3

I DECIDED TO TRY The Ritz job. Not because I wanted to learn how to cook or work under the direction of the famous Chef Antonio. It was because I'd heard the star actors and director for the film Pocket Money Pictures was making would, in all likelihood, stay at The Ritz. It might be the break I needed. Who knows what could happen? Lana Turner, the glamorous movie star of the 1940s, had been discovered sitting at the Top Hat Café in Hollywood. I know that because I read everything about movies I can get my hands on. This isn't Hollywood or the 1940s, and Lana Turner is dead now, but The Ritz dining room is a cut above a café soda fountain.

Although I'd be working in the kitchen, film stars and celebrities were always ducking into the hotel kitchens to get away from fans and autograph hunters. Maybe I'd be spotted by some talent scout or at least be asked to be a stand-in for some actor for a stunt. Anyway, I reasoned, I'd have a far better chance to be close to the film industry at The Ritz than working at Joe's Meatmarket, Pete's Autowreckers, or bagging groceries at Fletcher's Foods.

So I got my hair cut. I asked for a trim. I didn't have much money so Mom cut it for me. She was humming something as she worked on my hair.

"What's that tune?" I asked.

"Oh, it's from *The Barber of Seville*." She grinned. "Appropriate, don't you think?"

Mom sang in a trio. She has a pretty good voice and probably could have been a professional singer, but she was happy to sing just for fun.

I looked at my hair in the mirror in the kitchen. I gasped. "It's too short!"

"Nonsense," Mom said. "I've hardly cut any off. Look at how little hair there is on the floor. Anyway, if you don't like it, you can always go out and get a proper haircut at the barber and pay for it. This is free."

I stopped complaining. I guess she hadn't cut much off, and I didn't feel like paying ten bucks or more for getting just a trim.

Yesterday, when Mr. Shamberg had given us our job assignments in class, Celia let out a gasp and beamed with pleasure when she heard she'd be working at Pocket Money Pictures. Joe Straka got the job at Pete's Autowreckers and he promised to pay me back for the loss of my cap out of his first paycheque.

"Hey! Really high class," Leonard Wooley said as he clapped me on the back when he heard I'd got The Ritz job. He knew I'd had my heart set on Pocket Money Pictures and he was trying to cheer me up. "I'll bet you'll make a fantastic cheesecake. I'll come over to your place for dessert every night."

I presented myself at the reception desk of The Ritz at 4 p.m. but I had to wait in line. Everyone behind the desk was either on the phone or tapping away at computers as they checked guests in. I quickly scanned the huge lobby for possible film stars or directors, but I couldn't spot any obvious ones. Everyone looked pretty ordinary. An orchestra was playing soft music somewhere off to one side, in what I assumed must be the dining room. I wondered how long it would be before the diners in there were afflicted by my efforts at cooking.

I turned my attention to the deep, plush, blue carpeting that covered the lobby. It was so thick my running shoes sank into it and when I moved my feet they left footprints in the carpet for a few seconds. The footprints slowly disappeared as the carpet puffed back into place. It was really neat, and I tested out different techniques, pressing really hard with one foot and softer with the other to see if one footprint would last longer than the other. It did. Then I tried standing on the edge of my runners and made Xs.

"Do you have a reservation?"

Startled, because I was so engrossed with my carpet designs and hadn't noticed that the person who'd been in front of me had left, I glanced up at the woman behind the desk. She was frowning as she peered over the reservation desk to see what I was doing with my feet. I bet she thought I was cleaning my shoes on The Ritz's carpet. I felt myself blush.

"Um, no," I stammered. "I have an appointment with Ms. Capstone."

"Your name, please?"

"Harry. Harry Flanagan."

"Is she expecting you?"

"Um, yes. I'm here from Crestwood High, for the work experience program." When I said it, it sounded to me like I'd just been released from prison after serving twenty-five years for some terrible crime.

"One moment please." The woman picked up a telephone and spoke rapidly into it, giving me furtive glances all the time. It was as if she suspected I was about to revert to whatever criminal behaviour I'd committed in the past. When she put the phone down, she said, "Go down the hall on the right and take the elevator at the end of the hall. You'll find Ms. Capstone in the executive offices on the third floor."

"Thanks," I mumbled as I headed for the hallway.

I had to wait in an outer office for a while until I was shown into Ms. Capstone's office by her secretary.

Ms. Capstone was scary. She wasn't overweight but she was a large woman and she sat behind an equally large desk. I guessed her age was about thirty-five. Her dark, shoulder-length hair was covering one side of her face and was pinned back behind her ear on the other side.

She reminded me of somebody or something I couldn't quite pin down. I temporarily settled for undertaker, except her black formal suit had a red leather belt circling her waist, and her lipstick matched the red of her belt. But the strangest thing about her was her eyebrows, or at least the one full eyebrow I could clearly see and the bit of the other one that disappeared under her hair. They didn't grow over her eyes but shot up at a sharp angle from near the top of her nose and I guessed, if I could see both of them completely, they would form a large V across her forehead. But because her hair hid most of the one on the right side of her face, it looked like she was wearing a large checkmark. It looked like the ones Mr. Shamberg uses on our notebooks except that his checkmarks are usually in red. Ms. Capstone's was jet black. It took me a minute or two to figure out her eyebrows weren't real. They were painted on, and she must have plucked out all the little hairs from her real eyebrows. *Painful*, I thought.

She didn't smile, but the one eyebrow, totally visible, moved alarmingly on her head and indicated a chair in front of her desk. I sat. I was still wondering how she had such control over a fake eyebrow when she startled me by suddenly barking out a question.

"So you want to be a chef?" Her voice boomed and echoed off the walls of her office.

"Um. No. I mean yes." I almost said I really wanted to be a film director or at least an actor, and I had absolutely no interest in becoming a chef, but I guessed Mr. Shamberg had probably lied about my interest in cooking to get me this job. Our school program had very few spares and it was either this job or spend three afternoons a week up to my elbows in blood, like Leonard at Joe's Meatmarket. Or, like Joe Straka, scouring the muddy yard at Pete's Autowreckers, looking for matching hubcaps.

"So why do you want to be a chef?" Ms. Capstone asked me, and I couldn't help staring at the way her full eyebrow danced on her head, and the bit of the other one I could see darted behind her hair as if it had taken flight. Then I remembered what it was Ms. Capstone reminded me of. It was the spider I'd startled one summer when I was on holiday at Uncle Dan's in southern British Columbia, and I was helping him weed his rock garden. I'd pulled a bit of grass from between two rocks and a couple of black hairy legs popped out of the hole and were quickly followed by the other six, on which sat a shiny black round body. I'd jumped back in surprise and Uncle Dan had laughed. "Black widow," he'd said. "See the red mark on her underbelly? She has a poisonous bite and she kills and eats the male right after they mate."

I gulped, not because I thought Ms. Capstone was about to devour me — after all, we'd only just met — but because Mr. Shamberg told us we should be ready for a question like the one

Ms. Capstone had just asked. I'd practised the answer for weeks, but that was in the belief I would be interviewed by Pocket Money Pictures. I could give a dozen reasons why I wanted to work in the motion picture industry. I couldn't think of one reason why I would want to be a chef. Why would anyone?

I frantically racked my brain. I couldn't just say I liked food. Mr. Shamberg had gone over the objectives of the work experience program with us in class. What were they?

"I want to explore a career opportunity at the source," I blurted. It was the only objective I could remember, and as soon as I said it I knew it sounded phony, like some political slogan. "Oh, I have this letter of introduction." I fumbled in my pocket for the letter Mr. Shamberg had given me and placed it in front of Ms. Capstone.

"Hmm." Her eyebrows twitched as she looked down at it like it was some unworthy insect that had just landed in her web.

I waited anxiously while she read the letter. "It says here you have an inquisitive mind and are eager to learn." She looked at me. "Mr. Flanagan, being eager to learn is important, but I must stress that here at The Ritz we have a very high reputation. Nothing must be allowed to sully that reputation. The comfort and needs of our guests come first and foremost. Privacy is very important to our guests, and anything you learn of their comings and goings, their eating habits, and so on, must be kept in the strictest confidence. Do you understand?"

I nodded.

"This is the second year we have been associated with the work experience program and I must admit I had some reservations about continuing after what happened last year. But that's confidential. Now before you can start work here, you must present yourself at the security office on the second floor. I suggest you do that tomorrow, after you get a haircut.

You'll be given an identification tag you must wear at all times. Ask for Miss Marsden. After you've been photographed and given your tag, she'll direct you to where the kitchen is located. Chef Antonio will want to meet with you. He's very particular about who works in his kitchen. If he is busy you can ask for one of the sous chefs, Gustav Halterman or Walter Nakamura. But a haircut is the first thing you need."

I was about to protest I'd already got a haircut but Ms. Capstone's phone was ringing and she dismissed me with a twitch of her one full eyebrow, while the other one leaped for cover.

4

I WAS WALKING ALONG a back street not far from The Ritz, looking for a bus stop that listed the bus route I needed to get home, when I saw the sign, HAIRCUTS, FIVE DOLLARS. A bargain. I knew Mom was going to a practice with her singing group and wouldn't be home until late and she wouldn't have time to cut my hair again. I had six bucks in my wallet and I figured I'd better get another trim before I faced the great Antonio tomorrow.

I went in and was sitting in a chair with a red robe over me when I saw the sign on the wall: HAIR AND THERE BARBER SCHOOL — PRICE LIST. I gulped. I was in a barber school. That's why the haircut was only five bucks. The other two customers being worked on were an old lady who'd fallen asleep and a little kid who kept jerking his head and saying "ouch" every time his barber snipped a piece off his hair. The kid's dad was saying, "hang in there, Tiger. Mom's gonna love the way you look." His eyes met mine in the mirror. "His first time." He nodded in the direction of his kid, but I wasn't sure whether he meant his kid or the barber, and that got me really worried.

In the mirror I could see the guy who was about to cut my hair studying the back of my head and nervously snipping the air with his scissors.

"I just need a trim," I stammered. I hoped I wasn't his very first customer.

He nodded, then attacked my head with his scissors like he was conducting an orchestra. Hair was falling around me in clumps and every now and then a guy I assumed was the supervisor put down the magazine he was reading, got out of a barber chair where he was sitting, and came and inspected my head. He'd point to the back of my head and the guy cutting my hair would snip some more. The scariest part was when he put down his scissors and picked up a straight razor and started sharpening it on a strap. I hoped he wasn't going to fling himself on me like he had with the scissors. I closed my eyes when he pressed my head forward and I felt the scrape of the razor on my neck.

"All done." He whipped the robe off of me with a flourish and I opened my eyes and gasped. I was expecting to see a lot of my blood, but the whole robe was bright red. Then I remembered it was red to begin with. I felt the back of my neck as the trainee barber brushed hairs from my collar, and I was so relieved to discover I wasn't bleeding I gave him my whole six dollars.

When I got out on the street I realized I'd have to walk home. I knew I'd left my bus pass at home and I'd just spent my bus fare on a tip for a terrible haircut.

"What happened to your head?" Leonard Wooley asked as soon as I walked into class the next morning. "You get caught in another fire?"

"No. Just a fire sale on haircuts."

It was so embarrassing. Everyone kept glancing at me. I'd looked at the back of my head with a mirror as soon as I'd got home from the barber, and I knew what I looked like. There were bald spots up the back of my head and the top looked like it had been chewed on by rats while I slept. My chances of getting a bit part in the movie, which I'd heard was called *Funeral at Feng-t'ai*, were really hitting rock bottom. From what I'd heard, there were no characters who looked like they were escaped cons, or recovering from a bad case of ringworm.

I gritted my teeth when Mr. Shamberg asked if we'd all got to our assigned workplaces and how we'd made out, and Celia bubbled with excitement about how she'd bumped into the star, Johnny Random.

"And what will you be doing on the set?" Mr. Shamberg asked.

"Oh. They said I could be the best boy."

There were hoots of laughter from some of the guys and Celia blushed.

"Aren't they a little confused?" Dennis Wilton chortled. "I mean, how blind can they be?"

"It's what they call the electrician's helper in the movies," Celia was explaining in an embarrassed voice, "but I'm not sure what I'll be doing."

I'd stopped listening. *Best boy*, I thought. That meant her name would even appear in the credits. What a great opportunity and I'd missed out on it. Instead of rubbing shoulders with stars like Johnny Random, I'd be stuck in the bowels of The Ritz rubbing dirt off carrots.

"And how did you make out, Harry?" Mr. Shamberg was asking.

"Uh. Okay, I guess. I just went to the personnel office yesterday. I have to meet the chef today and I think I'll probably start at The Ritz tomorrow." I knew I didn't sound too enthusiastic.

Mr. Shamberg noticed. "It'll be fine, Harry. You'll probably really enjoy it. Chef Antonio has a great reputation."

* * *

I didn't know much about Chef Antonio's great reputation, but I quickly found out he had a terrible temper. I had stopped off at security on the second floor like Ms. Capstone had directed. There they'd snapped my picture and laminated it onto a security tag and pinned it on my jacket. Then they directed me to the kitchen.

I pushed open a swinging door and I found myself in the middle of a fierce argument. A big man with a bright red face, wearing a chef's hat, was yelling in French at a much smaller man. He punctuated each explosive phrase by flinging a handful of prawns into some bowls. (I didn't know they were prawns at the time. On my first day at The Ritz, I couldn't tell a prawn from a perogy.) Several other chefs or cooks were busy cutting or chopping vegetables, stirring pots on huge stoves and going about their business, trying to ignore the tirade that was going on.

The chef's voice rose almost to a scream, and a particularly violent fling sent prawns bouncing out of a bowl and onto the floor.

The small man said something in French, which brought another howl from the chef, who looked like he was ready to kill. I noticed one cook hastily move a collection of knives further away from the chef. Quickly grabbing up the bowls of prawns, the small man beat a hasty retreat through another swinging door as the chef flung one final handful of prawns at his retreating back.

I was still standing partway through the door into the kitchen, wondering if I should also retreat and come back later, when the chef turned and noticed me. His face changed quickly to a normal colour, like someone had turned off a light bulb inside his head.

"Yes?" he asked. "And what would you like?" He spoke English but with a decidedly French accent. I was relieved. This couldn't be Chef Antonio. Antonio was an Italian name, not French.

"I'm Harry Flanagan," I stammered, pointing to my security badge. "I'm looking for Chef Antonio. I'm from Crestwood High. I'm with the work experience program."

"Okay. You'll do. I am Chef Antonio. Be here tomorrow at 2 p.m. sharp." He strode off across the kitchen but turned just before I backed out the door and his voice boomed across the room. "But first get a haircut."

No one was home. I went into the bathroom, locked the door, and shaved my head. I figured that I had nothing to lose. My hair was a mess and everyone was staring at me in school anyway, so having a bald head wouldn't produce any more stares than I was getting now, and the bald bits on my neck wouldn't stand out anymore. And nobody at The Ritz would tell me to get a haircut.

I gaped at myself in the mirror. I hadn't realized I would look so different. I rubbed my hand over my smooth head and it felt weird. But there was nothing I could do about it now.

I unlocked the bathroom door and walked into the kitchen.

"Oh my," Mom was saying to herself, "Aunt Phyllis is coming to stay and she's arriving tomorrow." She looked up from the letter she had in her hand. Then she let out a shriek and flung the pages of the letter into the air.

I bent to pick up the pages as Mom collapsed onto a chair. "Oh Harry! It is you. You gave me quite a turn. I thought you were an intruder or burglar or something. What happened to your hair? You haven't been playing with fire again have you? I thought you had got over that stage long ago."

"No Mom. I just got fed up with everyone telling me to get a haircut. Does it look that bad?"

Mom studied me for a moment. Then she smiled and stood up and gave me a hug. "It's different. I'm sure I'll get used to it very quickly. When you were a baby you didn't have any hair and I thought you were beautiful. I used to kiss you on the top of your head. You're too tall for that now." She squeezed me harder. "But you're still my handsome little boy." She laughed. "Aunt Phyllis will no doubt have something to say and you'll have to put up with your father's comments. But you won't have him telling you your hair is too long and you look scruffy.

"Well, I'd better get busy and tidy up the spare room for Aunt Phyllis. She didn't say how long she is going to stay. You know how she just arrives at a moment's notice and disappears just as quickly. Your father won't be too happy though." Mom bustled off to the spare bedroom.

Aunt Phyllis is Mom's aunt. She's in her late sixties. She usually visits us about once a year, and it's a trying time for everyone.

* * *

In the huge kitchen at The Ritz, my guide, Kin Woo, studied me for a moment and then grinned. "How come you Caucasian guys all look the same? Old Chinese joke. First you need uniform. Come."

He led me through a door off the kitchen into a hallway and from there into a small locker room.

"What size are you? Medium, I guess." Kin rummaged in a cupboard in a corner of the room and pulled out a pair of white pants and a jacket. "Here. Try on these pants." Kin was a pretty good guesser. The pants were a perfect fit. The jacket buttoned up to the neck. Kin told me the first thing I had to do each day was to change into my uniform and wash my hands before coming into the kitchen.

"They fit okay, Harry? Good. Now you remember the number inside the jacket and pants. That will be your number from now on. You must check for your number when you come in. The laundry people hang all the clean uniforms here and you have to find your own."

"What about a hat?" I asked.

"No hat needed, Harry. Only if you have to work in dining room where customers can see you." Kin grinned. "Anyway, no chance of you getting hair in the soup. Maybe I give you Chinese name. Chan Yat Mao."

"What's that mean?"

"It really means One Haired Chan. But in Chinese it's a way of saying bald."

It turned out only Chef Antonio and the two sous chefs wore real chef hats. It was too bad because a chef's hat would have covered most of my bald head and, after the ribbing I'd taken all day, I was feeling very self-conscious.

It had started at breakfast. Dad hadn't seen me the night before. He'd been working late and I was in bed when he got home. I'd planned on leaving early before he got up, but Mom wouldn't let me leave without some breakfast. I was gulping down some cereal when Dad came into the kitchen.

"Holy Toledo! You get your head caught in the chicken plucker at The Ritz, or is there a bad case of head lice going around your school? Wait a minute. You're not turning into one of those skins heads or rocker punks or whatever they're called. I won't put up with that."

"Oh George, leave Harry alone," Mom scolded. "He's not turning into a skins head. It's *skinhead*, anyway. You've been bugging him to get a haircut for months and now he has."

"I didn't mean he had to go and look like that dead actor, what's his name. He was in *The King and I*. Yul Brimmer, that's it."

"His name was Brynner, Dad," I said. "Not Brimmer."

"Whatever."

"Aunt Phyllis is coming," Mom announced. I knew she was trying to get Dad to leave me alone and mentioning Aunt Phyllis was a sure way to do it.

"Aunt Phyllis! Not again. Wasn't she here only a month ago? Why is she coming so soon? Can't you talk her out of it? You know how she drives us all crazy. And she's crazy to begin with."

"It's been over six months since she was here," Mom said. "And she only stayed four days."

"It felt like six months to me," Dad grumbled.

I finished my cereal and hurried off to brush my teeth. Dad was still complaining about Aunt Phyllis as I waved to Mom, slipped out the door, and headed for school.

It was true Aunt Phyllis did drive us all a bit crazy, but it was Dad who really felt bugged by her the most. I usually found her just funny. Mom tolerated her, although she was always giving Mom unwanted advice about Mom's singing career. Aunt Phyllis had grown up in musical theatre and, although she'd had bit parts in a number of musicals, she always made them sound like leading roles. For years she'd been pushing Mom to get professional voice lessons and audition for some of the major roles in the musicals that came to the city. But although Mom loved the musicals, she didn't want a career on the stage. She was perfectly happy being part of her amateur trio. No matter how many times Mom insisted she was perfectly happy being part of her trio, that didn't stop Aunt Phyllis. She would carry on about how Mom was wasting her talent in such amateur productions and would claim some famous opera star or actor had only gone on to fame and fortune because they'd heeded her advice.

Although I'd wanted to leave the house early and escape from Dad, I decided it would be best if I arrived in school just as the bell rang. Then I wouldn't have to face the questions and questioning looks of every kid in the hallways. I'd get into class at the last minute and play it cool. That way I'd get most of the questions over with in one go.

I had a list of smart answers and was practising them in my head, like I was captured by aliens and they shaved my head because they experimented on my brain, or I've just been selected for the Olympic swim team and my coach said if I shaved my head I'd be sure to knock at least one second off the world record in the 400-metre freestyle.

Just as the bell rang I suddenly remembered the first class that morning was math with Ms. Cranshaw and it was unlikely that I'd get any of my witty answers off. Instead I'd be faced with a lecture on the evils of tardiness. I rushed in and dropped into my desk as Ms. Cranshaw was calling attendance. There were a few giggles and someone behind me hissed, "It's Sinéad O'Connor." I knew Sinéad O'Connor had let her hair grow back. Someone else whispered, "He's from *Star Trek*."

Ms. Cranshaw was staring at me. "Ah, a new student. I'm afraid you can't sit in that desk. It's Harry Flanagan's. Please come and sit here." She indicated a desk next to Celia Spendlove.

Was Ms. Cranshaw putting me on? Surely she knew who I was. I felt myself blush and I was sure even my bald head turned pink.

"Come forward, come forward," Ms. Cranshaw snapped. "We haven't got time to waste in this class. There's a lot to get through before the end of term. What is your name please?"

Ms. Cranshaw wasn't joking. She never joked. I noticed that today she was wearing her contacts instead of her glasses, something she rarely did. We all knew she couldn't see nearly as well with her contacts by the way she held the textbook close to her face. She really didn't recognize me.

She was waiting, still pointing to the desk beside Celia. Before I'd shaved my head I'd have given anything to sit next to Celia. The class was breaking up with laughter and Ms. Cranshaw was losing patience.

"Silence!" she yelled. "Now sit here and give me your name."

It was no use arguing. Ms. Cranshaw was obviously not going to wait for any explanation.

"It's Harry," I mumbled.

"I assume that's Harold." Ms. Cranshaw was carefully printing in her attendance list. The class was in hysterics behind me and I could see Celia was grinning like crazy. "And your last name?" Ms. Cranshaw went on.

"Flanagan."

"We already have a Harold Flanagan." Ms. Cranshaw was now peering at me. "What tomfoolery is this?" She'd finally recognized me.

"He's not *Tom Foolery*. He's Harry Flanagan," some wit howled from the back and the whole class shrieked with laughter.

Ms. Cranshaw slammed her text on the top of her desk. "Stop this at once," she hollered. "Turn to page seventy-nine. I want the entire page completed before the end of the period and, if there are any more outbursts, I'll assign another page for homework."

There were a few groans as the laughing stopped.

"As for you, Harold Flanagan," Ms. Cranshaw snapped. "I don't know what you are up to but I won't stand for any nonsense. I have my eye on you and I'll be watching you closely. In fact, this will be your desk for the rest of the year. Get your books and begin working, now!"

There were a few laughs when I stumbled over someone's foot on the way back to my old desk, but they were silenced by a glare from Ms. Cranshaw. I grabbed my books and dropped back into the desk beside Celia.

I kept my head down most of the period but a couple of times I glanced up to find Ms. Cranshaw was staring at me as if to make sure I really was Harry Flanagan. When she was satisfied, she set to work to carefully remove the name Harold that she'd added to her attendance list. Besides disturbances in class, Ms. Cranshaw's other pet peeve is to mess up the neatness of her attendance list.

Still, I guess things hadn't turned out all bad. I was sitting next to Celia. I sneaked a glance at her. She had her head down, working on one of the math problems. She stopped writing in her notebook as she sensed me looking at her. She kept her head down but turned it slightly in my direction. I could see she was smiling. Maybe it was a smirk of derision at my new appearance, but I hoped it just might be a friendly grin instead.

6

"THIS WILL BE YOUR station," Kin said. We were standing at what looked to me to be an ordinary counter with a sink.

"You know how to turn potatoes?" Kin asked.

"Sure. Roast potatoes. I get a big spoon and turn them over in the roasting pan when they're brown on one side," I said confidently. I'd seen Mom do it lots of times when we were having a roast surrounded by roast potatoes. I'd even done it a few times myself, when Mom asked me because she was busy getting dessert ready or something. The only trick was to make sure you didn't get splashed by the grease when you reached into the oven.

"Not that kind of turning." Kin grinned. "I show you. Back in a minute."

While I waited for Kin to come back I looked around the enormous kitchen. I hadn't expected so much noise and hustle and bustle. The whole place seemed to be in a state of mass confusion. There was so much going on, I wondered how anyone could keep track of what was happening. A waiter would suddenly appear, yell an order at no one in particular as far as I could tell, and then disappear, while others arrived to whisk away plates of steaming food or fancy desserts. A telephone seemed to ring constantly in the background.

At stations on either side of me, cooks and kitchen workers were chopping food or running giant electric blenders. Behind me, another group stirred hissing pots on the enormous stoves. At one end of the kitchen, huge dishwashers sloshed away and there was a lot of clatter as bus boys darted in, carrying dirty dishes.

"First you peel, then you turn." Kin plonked a huge box of potatoes on my station counter. "Like this." He whipped a potato out of the box, gave it a quick wash in the sink and, in a couple of swift strokes, it was peeled. "Now we turn. Turning means to give the potato a new shape. This way."

I watched carefully as Kin shaved off a bit here and a bit there and handed me a potato shaped like one I'd never seen before. It had eight sides. It looked easy enough.

"Now you try."

I grabbed a potato, washed it in the sink, peeled it and started in on the potato carving. It was much harder than I thought. By the time I got anything resembling an eight-sided potato, there wasn't much of it left.

"Okay. I show you again." Kin took another potato and I studied each cut as closely as I could. Then I tried one again. It didn't turn out much better than the first.

"Okay, you practise. I come back later. Gotta go and prepare sauce for special."

Kin was a first cook and had been with The Ritz for fifteen years. He'd told me Chef Antonio's real name was Antoine, but he preferred the name Antonio, as he thought it was a more fashionable name for a chef. I'd learned that the chain of command in the kitchen, after Chef Antonio, was the two sous chefs, then the first, second, and third cooks (I wasn't sure how many there were of each), then the kitchen help, some of them part-timers like me. In another section, away from the main kitchen, a smaller group handled outside catering for big private dinners or wedding receptions that weren't being held at the hotel.

I gritted my teeth as I tackled another potato. I wondered if it would take me fifteen years to learn how to turn potatoes like Kin. Why couldn't the potatoes just be washed and peeled? They weren't going to taste one bit better by hacking them into weird shapes. If potatoes were supposed to look like this, I thought, some agricultural experimental research station would find a way of growing potatoes that looked like that when they came out of the ground.

My third effort looked bigger and a bit better but when I counted the sides I found it had only six instead of eight. But what was the big deal anyway? I couldn't imagine anyone saying, "Waiter, take this back. This potato has two sides missing." Who would notice something like that?

Chef Antonio, that's who. He loomed over my shoulder, reached into the sink and grabbed one of my miniature potatoes, then tossed it back with a resounding clunk. "Marbles we don't need! Potatoes with nice shapes, yes, we can cook. But The Ritz cannot serve marbles. And hurry. These are needed right away!" He stomped off and then started yelling at someone at another station. "More salt, more salt."

I tried to speed up. I peeled and washed about half the box of potatoes and then tried again at turning them. I was slow, but I got better and a little faster. Kin came back to check on how I was doing. "Okay, Harry. Not to worry. You soon get the hang of it. Here. Another box."

I groaned. "More?"

"I do a few to help you out." Kin grinned and proceeded to whip through what was left of my first box.

I studied what he did as carefully as I could and tried to follow, but my potatoes never did turn out as good looking as his. When the first box was finished, he patted me on the back. "You're getting better. Hang in there. Gotta go now."

By the time I'd finished the second box of potatoes my shoulders were aching and I hadn't even finished half my shift, according to the clock on the kitchen wall.

Kin appeared at my station with a cart in tow. "New job. Sous chef says we need lots of melon peeled. Big party coming in tonight."

I gasped when I saw the cart was loaded with five cases of honeydew melons.

"Don't you just serve the melons in slices with the skin on?" I asked.

"Not at The Ritz. Melon balls, fruit plates, no skin. Not so bad as turning potatoes. You'll like it better."

By the time my shift was over and it was time to go home, I never wanted to see another honeydew melon again. I'd got them all peeled, but they were slippery and, in the process, I managed to drop a couple on the floor. As I scrambled to rescue them, I expected to hear a bellow from Chef Antonio but he was busy elsewhere, yelling at someone else.

When I got home, Mom greeted me with a cheery smile and the news that Aunt Phyllis wouldn't be arriving until the next day, because of some mix up with her ticket. "She said she'll take the airport bus into the city and make her way from downtown later. She said she had to make an important call on someone at a downtown hotel."

"She should stay there," Dad said. He was already eating supper.

"Now, George. I'm sure she won't stay here all that long. Sit down and have your supper, Harry, and tell us about your first day in your new job."

"Yeah," Dad said. "Maybe he can do the cooking from now on and Aunt Phyllis's stay will be even shorter."

Mom ladled out a large plate of her delicious stew and set it in front of me. "Ignore your father, Harry. When you finish your stew, I've got a special treat for dessert. I know you'll like it. They were on special at Fletcher's Food so I bought two."

I groaned as Mom placed a honeydew melon on the table.

"You've given the poor boy quite a turn there, mother." Dad laughed. "Me too, for that matter. I thought you'd served Harry's head on a plate for a minute."

"What's the matter, Harry?" Mom looked worried.

"It's okay Mom. Just don't ask me to peel it."

7

I WAS ALMOST LATE getting to The Ritz the next day because the bus got stuck in a traffic jam. When I got to the locker room and tried on the pants of my uniform, something was definitely wrong. They were huge. They would make a perfect fit for Chef Antonio. Maybe they were his. What if he came in and found me trying on his pants? In a panic, I whipped them off and checked the number — BK46. What was my uniform number? I desperately tried to remember it, but my mind had gone blank. Maybe it was 64.

I rummaged through the uniforms, looking for pants that seemed to be my size. I found a pair and checked the number on the tag inside — K16. Couldn't be mine. But I couldn't find anything else even close to my size and, if I went into the kitchen wearing my jeans, Chef Antonio would let me have it. I was making another frantic search when I was startled by someone asking, "Did you lose your pants,

Harry?" I whirled around and came face to face with Celia.

"What, what are you doing here?" I stammered.

"I had a couple of those rare spares. I work here part-time." She smiled. "I'm with outside catering."

"Did you quit the movie job or what?" I asked.

"No. I've had this part-time job at The Ritz for over six weeks. I work a couple of shifts a week or sometimes a bit more if they call me and I'm available. So what's your uniform number? Sometimes housekeeping gets the pants and shirts mixed up."

"I thought it was 46 but maybe it was 64. I'm not sure." I felt like a real dope and I knew I was blushing.

"Well, the shirt fits fine. What's the number on it?"

"Um …"

"Take it off and check if you can't remember. Then you might find the pants to match."

I felt like a dummy as I unbuttoned the shirt and took it off. "It's X16," I said, reading the tag.

Celia pointed to the tag and shook her head. "No, it's 91K. You read the tag upside down and that X is just a smudged K. K stands for kitchen, OC for outside catering, and BK for the banquet kitchen, upstairs. There is no X. Yours should be a K. Here's a pair of pants with the same number, K91. Housekeeping isn't always consistent about whether they put the letter before or after the number. They look like they might fit you. Gotta go." Celia grabbed a uniform off a hook and disappeared into a nearby washroom to change.

I whipped on the pants and shirt and hurried into the kitchen, not wanting to have to face Celia. I was so embarrassed.

I didn't see her again, and I spent most of my shift chopping a ton of celery. Chef Antonio came by and hollered at me, "Brunoise! Brunoise!" I wasn't sure what he meant. Was he yelling in French or was it just his accent? I tried to chop more quietly, but couldn't understand how my little bit of chopping noise could disturb anything. The rest of the kitchen noises were much louder. I was relieved when Kin came over and explained that Chef Antonio needed some celery diced very fine. *Brunoise* meant dicing the celery into two-millimeter squares. Kin showed me. The stuff I'd already chopped was to be used for soup stock. A short while later, Chef Antonio came by, and without a word, scooped the finely diced celery into a bowl and left.

With a half hour left on my shift, Kin asked me to help him set up a display at the entrance to the dining room. I was glad of the change. Celery chopping is not very exciting. Before we went into the dining room we had to put on chef hats, as we would be in public view.

Kin explained that every couple of weeks the display was changed to reflect some theme about food. The next two weeks would feature different kinds of squash.

The display table was just a short distance from the hotel check-in area off the lobby and, as I handed Kin different shaped and coloured squash, which he arranged artistically, I became aware of raised voices coming from the check-in counter.

"I'll have you know, young man, that I am very well known to Robert Rudsnicker and I know he would want to see me. Now, if you would just telephone his suite and let him know I am here."

"I'm sorry, madam," a male voice behind the desk explained patiently, "but we have a strict policy here that our guests cannot be disturbed unless we have been informed that a visitor is expected. I cannot even confirm that Mr. Rudsnicker is staying at this hotel and I can find no record of your name, madam, on the expected visitor list for any of our guests. I'm sorry. There's nothing I can do. It's a matter of security. Perhaps if you were to leave a written note?"

"Nonsense. Of course he's staying here. I'm an old friend, not some school girl looking for an autograph. A note indeed!" The woman's voice boomed out, full of indignation, and I thought I recognized it.

I handed Kin the last of the squash and glanced towards the check-in desk. I gasped as my worst fears were confirmed. It was Aunt Phyllis.

Even though she had used a blue rinse in her hair to make it look less yellow, she was still easily recognizable. There was no mistaking her. She always dressed dramatically, as if for a role in some play. A black cloak hung over her shoulders and was swept back to reveal a gold, almost metallic-looking dress, open along one side almost to her thigh. She wasn't very tall or very large, and she had a reasonably good figure for her age, but it was the way she stood and carried herself that made her stand out. She has a habit of throwing her head back, like she is about to give a rendition of some great Shakespearian soliloquy, or burst into full voice with some operatic aria. She gives the impression that she is in charge and will stand no nonsense. Now, her head was thrown back and she was glaring at the desk clerk, like she expected him to wilt before her.

"Okay, Harry, that's good enough for now," Kin said. "You can take off."

I mumbled my thanks and hurried back to the locker room to get out of my uniform. I hoped I wouldn't bump into Aunt Phyllis before I got home.

What I didn't know was that Aunt Phyllis was so put out with the desk clerk that she'd stomped off out of The Ritz, declining the offer of the doorman to whistle up a taxi for her. When I reached the bus stop, there she stood, at the back of a small line, fuming. A small suitcase sat on a tiny cart with wheels and she clutched another larger one in her hand.

The bus arrived just as I got to the line and the passengers started boarding. When Aunt Phyllis reached the door of the bus she just stood there, as if she expected the bus driver to step down and assist her with her bags. I don't think she rode on buses much.

What could I do? I suppose I could have turned and ran and caught another bus, but the bus driver was hollering, "Lady. Are you getting on or not?"

"Come on, Aunt Phyllis. It's me, Harry. Let me give you a hand with your bags." I made a grab for the suitcase in her hand but she snatched it away.

"How dare you? Unhand me! Harry indeed! I'd know my nephew anywhere. And he certainly isn't bald."

"Sorry, lady," the bus driver called. "Got a schedule to keep." The door slammed shut and the bus roared off.

"How dare he!" Aunt Phyllis snapped indignantly. "And you. You've made me miss my bus."

It took me another ten minutes to convince Aunt Phyllis it really was me and, when another bus arrived, she allowed me to help her with her bags and we got on. We got a glare from the driver at the sight of the suitcases and I heard him mutter, "This is a city bus, not a Greyhound."

We got him even more frustrated when Aunt Phyllis thrust a twenty dollar bill at him and said, "Two please," and I had to search for the exact change to pay for both of us, which resulted in us holding up the passengers behind us.

The bus was almost full but we found a seat near the back. I stowed Aunt Phyllis's bags under our seat as the other passengers boarded and then there was standing room only.

Aunt Phyllis was indignant over her treatment at The Ritz, and was still going on about it. She hadn't even given me a chance to explain why I happened to be there. I think she assumed I'd been sent to meet her. With the bus being so crowded, I was glad Aunt Phyllis didn't pursue her questions about my bald head. She always talked like she was performing on the stage for an audience and, as the bus headed out of downtown, I knew every passenger on the bus was listening to Aunt Phyllis. Not one other person on the bus was talking.

"And furthermore," Aunt Phyllis went on, "Robert Rudsnicker and I go way back. It was because of me he got his first break in films. He had this dreadful stammer, you see. Hopeless, if you expect a career on the stage or in films. I cured him of it and he got his first break. Of course, he never was a great actor. His forte is directing. That's where he really shines. He's directing a film right here, you know. I'm sure he'll want to use me in some dramatic role once he knows I'm here. Oh my goodness! Maybe it's a good thing I didn't get to see him this afternoon. I'm not properly dressed."

I could feel every eye on the bus swivel to stare at Aunt Phyllis and I slumped lower in my seat.

"Aunt Phyllis," I hissed, "everyone is listening."

Everyone, I was sure, heard me. Everyone except Aunt Phyllis.

"Yes. How dreadful. I was in such a rush to get to the airport this morning. I'm so glad Robert didn't see me. I've forgotten to put on my bra."

I squirmed as chuckles rippled inside the bus. I glanced across the crowded aisle and pretended to be interested in an ad pasted above the window. Maybe I could pretend I didn't really know this crazy lady beside me. The ad was just as embarrassing. It was for ladies' underwear. I glanced down the aisle towards the front of the bus. I was mortified to see Celia standing among the passengers in the aisle. She was grinning from ear to ear, like everyone else.

8

I was eating breakfast the next morning when Dad came into the kitchen, complaining that he hadn't been able to shower because Aunt Phyllis was still in the downstairs bathroom and had been there for nearly an hour.

"Why didn't you use the shower in the main bathroom?" Mom asked.

"Because I always use the one downstairs. The shower in the other one just trickles."

"Then it's time we got it fixed. You can't blame Aunt Phyllis."

"I could have showered if she wasn't taking so long putting on her makeup," Dad grumbled. "I have an early shift at Luxottica today."

Dad had worked on the assembly line at Luxottica Lighting since before I was born. He'd been disappointed when he'd found out I wasn't interested in applying for the work experience job there.

"How long can it take to slap on a bit of lipstick and powder, anyway? Not that it will do her any good," Dad continued.

"Now George. There's no need to be unkind," Mom said.

"I'm sure she's just hogging that bathroom deliberately. She knows I like to use the shower in that one."

"Good morning, George." Aunt Phyllis bustled in, followed by a waft of perfume. She was dressed in tight stretch black slacks and a gold, black-spotted blouse that looked, to me, like a leopard skin. "Sorry I missed you last night, George. I hear you were working late and I was very tired, so I went to bed early. I need my beauty sleep, you know."

"You can say that again," Dad mumbled, just loud enough for me to hear. He was staring at Aunt Phyllis's blue hair and, although Mom gave him a warning look, he couldn't resist commenting, "Did you get a starring role in a blue movie, or a job singing the blues?"

Aunt Phyllis gave him a frosty look as she stirred the coffee Mom placed in front of her. "Actually, George, it was a small French opera, set in the time of Louis the Sixteenth. He was the king of France, you know, George. Not one of those wrestlers you watch on that horrible TV program of yours."

I left for school at that point, with Mom trying to keep the peace.

I didn't see much of Celia in school anymore, except in Ms. Cranshaw's math class. Our work experience schedules had changed our timetables quite a bit for this semester. Celia was at Pocket Money Pictures most mornings and I left in the early afternoon for The Ritz.

When I got there that afternoon, Kin told me that he had a new job for me, and introduced me to Mario and Helga. They worked in room service and today they were short one person. Because of the film people staying in the hotel, they were very busy.

"All work experience," Kin grinned. "Better than chopping celery. Mario and Helga will show you what to do, okay?"

"I have to go and get some more chicken breasts. You show him, Helga." Mario, a short, dark-haired guy, scurried off, looking harried.

Helga nodded. She was an older lady with large brown eyes and a friendly smile. "Okay, Harry," she said. "When we get a phone call from one of the rooms, we answer the phone here. We write out the order on the bill. Then, we punch in the order here on this machine, and it shows up in a machine in the kitchen. While we wait for the food to be prepared, we set up the tray and one of these carts. The hot food goes underneath the cart in a hot box, so it stays warm." The phone rang and Helga answered it. I heard her repeat, "A club sandwich with fries and no gravy, and a spinach salad. Room 1104. Very good, sir."

She turned to me. "Okay. While I punch this order in, set up a tray on a cart — um, it needs flowers, water, a bun, and cutlery." The phone rang again. "Room service." Helga again repeated the order as she wrote it down. "A steak sandwich. Medium rare. A green salad. What kind of dressing? French. And a baked potato. Very good, sir. About fifteen minutes." She hung up. "Another tray, Harry. Don't forget the butter." She waved towards the tray I'd started preparing as she began punching in the orders on the machine.

I wasn't sure where to find everything and it took me a bit of time. The cutlery was wrapped in napkins on a counter, and I found the butter and buns okay. Did you get a bun with a steak sandwich? I guessed not. The flowers. Where were they? Helga had disappeared. The phone rang. I hesitated. Should I answer it? After the third ring I thought I'd better.

"Uh. Room service," I said nervously. What if I messed up the order?

It was a woman's voice. "Yes. I'd like to order a bottle of Chablis, French, of course, and a small cheese, brie, I think, would be best."

I frantically scribbled the order down and repeated it back like Helga had, although I'd no idea if I'd spelled Chablis and brie right. "Oh, the room number?" I'd almost forgotten to ask.

"Room 2014. Mr. Rudsnicker's suite."

I mumbled my thanks as the woman hung up.

Mr. Rudsnicker's suite, she'd said. The film director. Maybe this was my big chance, if I got to do the delivery. I'd get to meet him and maybe have a chance to talk to him.

Helga came back then, carrying some food, and rearranged the stuff I'd started to put on the trays. I told her about the order.

"Mario is taking a long time. You'll have to deliver it. I have to deliver these two orders. Go into the bar and get the wine, and ask for the cheese in the cold side section in the kitchen. I'll have the cart ready when you get back. The wine goes in the ice bucket. I'll put it on the cart. I'll make up the bill. Make sure the guest signs it, and bring it back."

I hurried off, leaving Helga arranging things, but it took me a few minutes to find the bar, get the wine from a busy bartender, and then find the cold food section of the kitchen. Luckily, I bumped into Kin and he showed me where to get the cheese. When I got back to room service, Helga was gone but the tray and cart were ready with wine glasses, ice bucket, and flowers. The bill slip was all made out. I had a moment of panic when I saw the corkscrew. I'd never opened a bottle of wine before. I would probably be expected to open and pour it.

I shoved the wine into the ice bucket, grabbed hold of the cart and headed for the elevator. The cart was heavier than I expected. It was just my luck to get one that didn't work properly. The same thing happened every time I went grocery shopping with Mom. The cart I picked always seemed to want to go in a different direction than the way I wanted it to go.

I made it into the elevator and pressed twenty. I glanced at the bill Helga had made up to check the number — 2014. I mustn't forget to get it signed by Robert Rudsnicker. I wondered if I'd even get to see him. It was a woman who'd phoned the order to room service. Maybe she'd meet me at the door and I wouldn't even get inside. But what if I did? What would I say to Robert Rudsnicker? I could tell him how I'd admired the last film he'd directed, *East of the Okavango*. It was a big adventure film set in Africa. He'd won an Academy Award for best direction. Maybe I'd get a chance to tell him how much I wanted to act and direct. I hadn't any more time to think about what I was going to say because the elevator door opened and I was on the twentieth floor.

I was startled to see a man in a suit, sitting on a chair opposite the elevator, reading a newspaper. He put the paper down, glanced at the identity card pinned to my shirt, gave me a nod, and went back to reading his paper. I guessed he must be with hotel security.

I pushed my wobbly cart down the carpeted hallway. There were only a few rooms on this floor, so the suites had to be huge. I found 2014 and rapped nervously on the door.

There was no answer, so I rapped again. The door opened suddenly and I was face to face with a very sleepy-looking Robert Rudsnicker.

"Roo-room service, sir," I stammered and I pushed my cart through the doorway.

Robert Rudsnicker yawned and then a puzzled look crossed his face. "Roo-room service. I da-da-don't remember or-ordering fr-from roo-room service."

At first, I thought he was mimicking me. Then, to our astonishment, my cart gave a sudden heave as something or someone tried to extricate themselves from the bottom level. A head bobbed out, a blue head. Then, with an awful crash, the whole cart tipped over, sending an avalanche of ice from the ice bucket across the carpet, to be quickly followed by the wine, cheese, the flowers, and everything else on the tray.

I was so startled I jumped back into the hallway. Then, with a great deal of thrashing and heaving, Aunt Phyllis scrambled out from the toppled cart. Before I could move or say anything, one of her thrashing legs caught the open door, slamming it shut in my face.

I stood there, dumbfounded, as the security guard raced up to me. "What happened?" he hollered.

I didn't know what to say. Inside the room I could hear Aunt Phyllis's voice saying, "Oh Robert, you have that nasty stammer back again."

I stepped aside as the security guy rapped on the door and it was opened again by Robert Rudsnicker.

"It's okay," he said. "Oh. Here." He thrust the room service bill at the security guy, who passed it to me as Robert Rudsnicker closed the door again.

I don't think Aunt Phyllis knew it was me she'd used to gain access to Robert Rudsnicker. If the hotel found out, I was sure to be fired.

As I headed for the elevator, the puzzled security guard followed, mumbling, "I'm sure that's the same broad I threw off this floor earlier. There's no accounting for these film types. I guess I'd better report it, in case there's any ramifications. I can't understand how she got in there."

I didn't want to think of the ramifications if the hotel found out that Aunt Phyllis and I were related.

9

AUNT PHYLLIS WAS BEAMING. "As soon as Robert Rudsnicker knew I was trying to reach him, he had me shown to his suite right away."

I spluttered in my bowl of Rice Krispies. Some went down the wrong way and I started choking.

Aunt Phyllis didn't notice. She went right on talking. Lying would probably be a better word.

"He was rather upset, in fact, that the hotel security staff had tried everything to prevent me from contacting him. He was delighted to see me and was grateful I was able to get him working again on getting rid of that stammer of his. He'd forgotten everything I'd taught him. It's all in the breathing, you see."

I was still trying to breathe myself. The Rice Krispies were still going snap, crackle, and pop in my windpipe. Mom poured me a glass of orange juice and shoved it towards me.

I gulped some of it down, and had almost relieved my choking, when Aunt Phyllis said, "Over a bottle of Chablis, Robert and I discussed a small part for me in the film, *Funeral at Feng-t'ai*, that he's directing. He remembered Chablis was my favourite and he'd already ordered it from room service before I'd reached his suite. He's very thoughtful."

"Sip the juice more slowly, don't gulp it," Mom said, clapping me on the back as my choking changed to a fit of coughing.

"So what does this mean?" Dad asked. "Will you be taking up residence in The Ritz now that you're a star, or what?"

"Well, no. Not exactly. I'll stay on here for a while."

I heard Dad groan, but Aunt Phyllis didn't seem to notice.

"Robert wants me to continue helping him with his breathing exercises for a few days. He's been having a terrible time with the co-star, Johnny Random. That's what brought Robert's stammer back, all the stress. Johnny Random's just got too big for his boots since he won the best actor award last year. Robert would like to replace him, but the film studio signed a contract that would cost them millions if Robert fired him, and of course Johnny Random knows it. The owners of Pocket Money Pictures hired Robert because they know he always strives to keep a film within budget, but they made a big mistake when they hired Johnny Random."

"So what's your part, then?" Dad asked. "The one this director fella promised you. What's his name again? Sounds like a dirty laugh." Dad laughed at his own joke.

"It's Rud-snicker," Aunt Phyllis snapped, as she stressed the first part of the director's last name. "Robert Rud-snicker."

"Well, I was close anyway," Dad went on. "I read in the paper this is one of those big battle movies in ancient China, with a big mob laying siege to some castle. That's a far cry from your last role in that French opera thing, unless you're going to play a geisha or something, entertaining the warlords. But with blue hair, I dunno." Dad mumbled the last bit, although I'm sure Aunt Phyllis heard him and chose to ignore the remark. "It beats me why they aren't filming the thing in China. They'd have a lot more Chinese to choose from."

"A good part of the film will be made in China," Aunt Phyllis replied.

"Oh! And the bad part here?" Dad couldn't control his laughter.

Aunt Phyllis frowned. "Sometimes, George, your humour is very juvenile. You know I wasn't fooled for one minute by that rubber lizard thing you hung on top of the shower curtain."

I gave a gasp, or what would have been a gasp if I wasn't still coughing and trying to sip the orange juice at the same time. I succeeded in snorting some of the juice up my nose. Aunt Phyllis had to be talking about Ralph. We didn't have any rubber lizards in the house, as far as I knew. I tried to glare at Dad, but I wasn't very successful because my coughing and choking had filled my eyes with tears.

I finally got my coughing under control enough to struggle to my feet to go check on Ralph and make sure he was okay.

Aunt Phyllis was still talking. "Most of the film, I believe, will be shot in China, but then it's easier to shoot the castle siege itself here, where there is more space. China has become far more crowded since the late 1800s, which is, I believe, the era when the actual event took place."

I couldn't believe it. Here was Aunt Phyllis hardly here one day, and, if what she said was true, she'd already landed a part in the movie. But how much was true? She'd lied about being invited to Robert Rudsnicker's suite. She'd lied about him ordering the wine before she got there. She was the one who had ordered it. I'd taken the order myself. Still, Robert Rudsnicker hadn't thrown her out. Maybe she had been promised a part. If so, I was the one who'd pushed her into it, so to speak.

I found Ralph dozing on the top of the shower rail. He opened one eye and looked at me for a moment, then closed it and went back to sleep.

"Lucky for you you didn't move when Aunt Phyllis was in here," I said to him, as I pried him off the rail. I had a hard time doing this, as he didn't want to be disturbed, and clung to the rail as hard as he could. "Come on, Ralph. Cooperate. You're lucky to be alive. If Aunt Phyllis had thought you were real, she might have freaked out and flattened you with the shampoo bottle."

I spent the morning in school thinking of ways I could get to meet Robert Rudsnicker myself, without throwing ice and flowers all over his hotel suite floor or having crazy old ladies jump from beneath room service carts. Would I get a chance to deliver something to his room again? It was unlikely. But if I did, would the fact that Aunt Phyllis was my great aunt influence Robert Rudsnicker into giving me a job as an extra? Storming a castle sounded far more exciting than chopping celery.

An announcement over the P.A. from Mr. Shamberg that work experience students should remember to get their weekly employment activity and time record sheets signed by their supervisors at the place of their employment started me scrabbling in the desk to look for my form. Unfortunately this was in Ms. Havershaw's class.

"Surely you haven't got that horrible reptile back here again," she shrieked.

"No, no," I said hurriedly. "I'm just looking for my time record sheet for work experience."

"Well, whatever zoo has employed you," Ms. Havershaw smirked at her joke, "will have to wait until math class is over. Those rat-scrabbling noises you are making are causing a disturbance."

"Sorry. I found it." I pulled the somewhat crumpled form out of the desk and held it up.

"Good. Good. Now perhaps we can get back to the topic at hand."

I caught Celia's eye as I bent over my math text. She smiled. I wondered how things were going on the movie set. I also wondered why Robert Rudsnicker was in The Ritz in the middle of the afternoon if he was shooting the film. If I got a chance, I'd ask Celia what was going on.

I didn't get a chance. When math class ended I couldn't find my form again and I started another search. By the time I found it on the floor, the form had a perfect imprint of some guy's muddy boot. I rushed off to Mr. Shamberg's office to get a new form but he wasn't there. By the time I found out he'd left the school, I'd missed my regular bus. I was going to be late at The Ritz.

I did my best to clean off my employment activity sheet, but it didn't help much. I changed into my uniform as quickly as possible and rushed into the kitchen to find Kin and get my assignment for the day. I couldn't see him anywhere. Everyone looked really busy.

"Somebody get that pot roast out of the oven, or it will be burnt, Cajun style." It was Chef Antonio. I hadn't noticed him before. He was standing not far from me, kneading some kind of dough, and his hands were covered in flour.

Nobody moved. Everyone, except me, was busy. I hesitated, but only for a moment.

"Somebody get that pot roast!" Chef Antonio roared, and glared pointedly at me and at the oven in question.

I pulled open the oven door. The huge pot with a lid was steaming and bubbling away, and a blast of heat hit me in the face. If I hadn't shaved my head I'm sure my hair would have been singed.

"*Vite! Vite!*" Chef Antonio yelled.

I didn't know what that meant, but I thought I'd better do something. I looked around desperately for something to grab the pot with, and someone tossed me what looked like a piece of an old bathrobe. I grabbed it, covered my hands with it, and reached into the oven for the pot. I hadn't expected it to be so heavy and my arms sagged under the weight. Unfortunately, the make-shift pot holder was indeed a piece of an old hotel bathrobe and several loose threads around the edges immediately ignited from the oven burner. I staggered back with the heavy pot and it looked like my hands were going up in flames. I spotted a counter to dump the pot on, but before I could hoist it up high enough, one of my hands slipped.

I tried desperately to hang onto the pot with one hand before it hit the floor. I wasn't successful. I wasn't strong enough. The free end of the pot bounced as it hit the floor, just as a pair of large feet loomed in front of me. For a second I thought, those white pants look a bit strange with brown cuffs. Then, to my horror, I realized I'd slopped brown gravy over the shoes and white pants. I didn't need to look up to check the owner. I knew. I tried to look on the bright side. The white pants may look bad, I thought, but at least the shoes were brown to begin with.

10

ALL THE CHOPPING AND mixing noises faded, then ceased altogether. The whole kitchen seemed to be waiting with bated breath. The only sounds came from the hissing pots on the stoves and a chugging dishwasher. In a daze, I sensed a pair of hands swoop up the pot off the floor and a pair of feet stomp on my flaming bathrobe.

I steeled myself for the explosion. It came, but not the way I expected. Like watching a movie in slow motion, I saw Chef Antonio look down at his pant cuffs, pick a speck of gravy off on the end of his finger and put it to his lips.

His face suddenly turned bright red. "More salt!" he bellowed. "More salt."

He glared around the kitchen at the cooks who suddenly became very interested in getting on with the preparation of the food. Mixers started to whir and chopping sounds took on a particular frenzy.

Chef Antonio turned on his heel and walked away as I caught sight of Kin beckoning to me. I hurried towards him, grateful that Chef Antonio had, for the moment at least, lost interest in me.

Kin was grinning from ear to ear. "You trying to get on good terms with Chef Antonio?"

"I guess that's the end of my job here," I groaned.

Kin was still grinning. "Don't worry. Chef Antonio has a temper. Sometimes he explodes, sometimes not. Today was your lucky day. Chef Antonio is more worried about taste. For him, everything needs lots of salt. His secret recipe."

"Well, he's not going to forget me spilling the gravy on his pants because today I have to get him to fill in my employment activity sheet." I pulled the grubby form out of my shirt pocket and showed in to Kin. "What's he gonna say about me when he fills this in?"

"Not much to fill in on this form," Kin said. "Mostly just what jobs you've been doing and number of hours."

"But what about the bit on the bottom?" I pointed. "What about 'observed strengths' and 'weaknesses'? And what about 'overall performance rating'? Where it says 'circle one: unsatisfactory, below average, average, above average, and outstanding'. And then there's supervisor's comments. What's he gonna say there? One word … *fired!*"

Kin put his chin in his hand and studied the form.

"Hmm. Maybe under 'observed weaknesses' he should say 'needs to develop stronger wrists for heavy pots.' And under 'observed strengths,' 'has burning desire to handle job. Really fired up.'" He burst out laughing.

"It's not funny, Kin."

"You worry too much, Harry. Chef Antonio hates filling in forms. And anyway, who tells you what to do every day?"

"Well, you do."

"So. Who do you think will fill in this form? I am really your supervisor, so, no problem. Anyway, no way you will get fired. We are very busy now with the hotel full and Mother's Day coming soon. Chef Antonio will just change his pants. Accidents happen in kitchen often."

I let out a sigh of relief. "Thanks, Kin."

"Oh, I almost forgot. Everything very busy right now. If you'd like to make a few extra bucks, outside catering is looking for extra help for private party tomorrow night. You interested?"

"Sure. I could do with the extra cash." And I'd get to work with Celia. She was sure to be working if they were short-handed.

"Good," Kin said. "You stay here after work. Bring a white shirt and your best pants. I'm not sure if you'll work as waiter or help with food. Henry Nicholson, he'll tell you. He's in charge of outside catering."

I spent the rest of the day turning carrots for Mother's Day — four hundred of them. I wondered how many mothers would show up at The Ritz and if they had anything to do with choosing the menu. Were mothers the same everywhere? Maybe, I thought, Chef Antonio's mother had told him to eat carrots when he was a kid because they were supposed to be good for his eyesight or something. By the time I'd finished all those carrots I think my eyesight was failing. I felt dizzy from the blur of orange in front of my eyes.

Before I left Kin brought me my completed employment activity sheet. He had made a photocopy, so the footprint wasn't so noticeable, and he'd given me a pretty good report.

I left for school early the next day before Aunt Phyllis was up. I didn't think I could stand listening to her go on about the role she was going to get in the movie. But I had a more important reason for leaving early. I caught up with Celia in the hall. I wasn't sure what to say to her. We hadn't talked much, except that time my pants hadn't fit me at The Ritz, and that was not exactly a topic I wanted to recall. So I just blurted out, "I'll be working with you tonight. I've been asked to help out with outside catering. They needed extra help."

"Oh." Celia seemed surprised. "It's the reception at city hall tonight."

"The reception? City hall?"

"Yeah. Don't you know what it is? The mayor and council are throwing a party to thank the film company for choosing our city to make the movie. It means a lot of money will be spent here. This is the first time I'll be able to mingle with the stars. I saw Johnny Random once, but I've hardly seen any others. I'm doing my best to stay out of the way of the sleazy electrician. He's always looking at me. He gives me the creeps. Just like that lizard of yours." Celia grinned.

"Sorry about Ralph," I mumbled.

Celia gave me a puzzled look. "How did you know the electrician's name?"

"I don't. That's the name of my iguana."

Celia burst out laughing. "How appropriate. I can even see the resemblance. Sorry, I'm insulting your lizard. I know you're really into films and, for a minute there, I thought maybe you not only knew the names of all the stars, but the names of the film crew as well." She continued laughing.

"So, apart from the electrician, Ralph, how's it going on the film set?"

"Actually, it's really boring. Working at the reception will be a nice change. Most of the time they have me running around delivering stuff or making coffee, but tomorrow I have to finish hanging up more bits of tinfoil. I've already spent the last few days hanging up hundreds of bits of the stuff. It's to simulate waves twinkling on the ocean."

"The ocean? But we're nowhere near the ocean," I said.

"I know that. That's why there's so much tinfoil. It hangs on bits of fishing line in front of a big photographic blue backdrop."

I couldn't believe I was having such a long conversation with Celia, but I must have sounded like a real whiner when I heard myself saying, "You're lucky. It can't be nearly as boring as turning carrots."

"Well, the set does look really neat. I think they're hoping to start shooting sometime next week. But things are behind a bit, so everyone is scrambling. They asked me to work this Saturday."

"Oh." I was envious about Celia's job, and I guess she noticed.

"Look," Celia said. "I know you wanted the job with the film company, but believe me, so far it hasn't been very exciting. You'll have a far better time at the reception tonight at city hall. Look," she hesitated, "if you're interested I could get you a pass and show you around the set tomorrow if you like. That is, if you're not doing anything."

"Great!" I said. "I'd love to see it. Thanks!"

"It's a long way out of the city. I'm supposed to start work at eleven. Everyone working on the film who's staying at The Ritz rides out in limos. Usually I get picked up in a small bus but tomorrow I have to catch a local bus. Want to meet me at the corner of Hurst and Gibson tomorrow at nine, and I'll have a couple of hours to show you around?"

"I'll be there."

"See you, then. Oh, and see you tonight." She smiled and hurried off to her first class.

I was excited. I couldn't believe my luck. Not only had I practically got a date with Celia, but I was going to be given a tour of the set. That was much better than just seeing her at the reception, where no doubt we'd be so busy we probably wouldn't even have a chance to talk. And she'd said that at the reception I'd get to rub shoulders with some of the stars. Things were looking up. This could be my golden opportunity.

I was glad I'd got up early and shaved the fuzz off my head this morning. It was beginning to look a bit weird. Dad had been up early too, to beat Aunt Phyllis to the shower. When he'd noticed my freshly shaved head he'd said, "And how's Confucius this morning?"

I think Confucius is the only Chinese person Dad has ever heard of. I didn't have a clue what Confucius might have looked like, but if Dad thought I looked somehow Chinese, it couldn't hurt my prospects for getting a bit part in the movie. It was, after all, a movie about a Chinese peasant uprising. Still, I thought, not many Chinese my age were bald. Maybe my long, dark hair would have given me a better chance. But it was too late now.

11

AT THE RITZ I was still helping to prepare for Mother's Day. This time it was zucchini. A mountain of the stuff. I'd hate to take my mother out for a Mother's Day dinner at The Ritz.

Just before quitting time, the outside catering crew arrived, led by a small dapper man. He carried a checklist and scurried around checking on dishes and desserts that had been prepared previously, making sure there was the right number of everything.

I was turning the last zucchini of the day when he came over with a red-haired guy in his twenties. "You're Harry? You're helping us out tonight. I'm Henry Nicholson and this is Bruce. He'll help you out. Follow what he does and you won't go wrong. If he's busy, ask one of the girls." He nodded towards three young women, who looked to be in their twenties, and Celia, who came in just then and gave me a wave. "You have a white shirt?" Mr. Nicholson asked.

I nodded.

"Good. Here's a white jacket. I think it will fit okay. Take it with you. Okay everybody. We're taking the food over to city hall, so it all has to be loaded in the van. When we get there, the food to be cooked can be taken straight into the kitchen. That's the food in the aluminum containers. I'll oversee the preparation of the hot food. The rest can be set out on tables — this is mostly a self-serve, buffet-style event. All of you will have to help serve canapés and city hall is, I believe, providing champagne. You won't have to serve drinks. City hall is organizing the bar service and waiters. All the dishes, cutlery, and so on are already there. We have some low-calorie desserts already prepared, but we are also providing crêpes flambé for those who request it. The hot food has to be ready for 6:30 p.m., but the canapés and snacks will be served first, before the speeches and introductions. We've got a lot to do people, so let's get on with it."

I hurried into the locker room and changed my shirt and pants and put on the white jacket. It fit. Then, with Bruce giving me instructions, I helped carry the containers of food out the back door of The Ritz into a large van parked in the alley. There seemed to be an awful lot of food. As soon as the van was loaded, Henry Nicholson jumped in behind the wheel and I followed Bruce and the others to a van further down the alley. Bruce drove.

I was the last one in the van and I found myself sitting on a short bench seat beside a woman called Marcie. Joanne and Dawn sat behind me and Celia was sitting on a single seat by herself at the back. Bruce made the introductions.

"So tonight, Joanne," Marcie said, laughing, "we get to mingle with Hollywood's finest." I wasn't sure if she was laughing at her remark or at my head, which I could sense she was staring at.

"Yeah," Joanne replied. "Hey, you know, Marcie, maybe I'll be discovered. I wonder if Johnny Random will be there. I read in *Tattle Tale* that his big romance with Claudia Kasperitis is off."

"You can't believe a thing you read in that rag," Dawn said. "Is that why you wore your mini? A good thing Henry didn't notice. You know how he is about proper dress."

"It is a proper dress," Joanne retorted. "Anyway, I've always fancied myself in the movies. And you never know your luck. Wasn't Bianca Bloodworth discovered sitting at a drug store soda fountain?"

"I dunno," Marcie said.

"Actually, it was Lana Turner," I said, turning my head to look back at Joanne.

"Who?" Marcie asked. All three women stared at me and I felt myself blush.

"Lana Turner," I repeated. "In the drug store, except it wasn't a drug store. It was in a café."

"Never heard of her," Dawn said. "Must have been before my time."

"It was," I said.

"What was?"

"Lana Turner. Before your time. It was in the 1940s."

"How old are you?" Marcie asked. She was staring at my head again. "I know you're bald and all that, but you don't look very old yourself. How do you know all this?"

"I read a lot about movies," I mumbled.

"Hey, Celia should know. She's working part-time for the movie company," Marcie said. "Hey Celia, will Johnny Random be there?"

"I've no idea. I've only seen him once."

"So what do you really do on that movie set, anyway?" Joanne asked. "Come on. Give us the scoop, Celia."

Joanne, Dawn, and Marcie broke into gales of laughter and I felt embarrassed for Celia. I guessed the three women didn't know that Celia and me knew each other.

"Mostly I just make coffee and deliver stuff," Celia said.

"Hmmph. More catering," Joanne said. "Well, if there are any producers, or whatever they're called, I should meet, be sure to introduce me. I'm tired of outside catering. I need a bit more excitement in my life."

"Here we are, everyone," Bruce called as he pulled the van to a stop.

"Remember, Joanne," Marcie said, laughing, "don't believe everyone you meet in here is a Hollywood producer waiting to make you a star."

There was a lot of joking and giggling as they scrambled out of the van, but they settled down when Mr. Nicholson started handing out the food containers from the back of the other van.

Inside city hall, a large room had been prepared with long tables covered in white tablecloths along the sides of the room. Plates and cutlery were stacked on the end of each table. The centre of the room was filled with round tables and chairs. A podium was set up at the front.

Only the barman and a couple of waiters were in the room, but we had barely got the cold food set out on the side tables when people began to arrive. I followed Bruce's lead in setting out the food and the others did the same.

Henry Nicholson appeared in the doorway of the kitchen and beckoned. When we were all in the kitchen, Mr. Nicholson said, "I see the room is already filling up and they've started serving drinks. A lot of them are reporters and they're a hungry lot. Better get those canapés out and circulate before they start on the desserts. The hot food will be another half hour."

Each of us picked up a couple of plates filled with little crackers covered in all sorts of fancy stuff that I couldn't recognize, and carried them into the reception room. I was surprised at how full the room was.

I spent the next half hour scurrying back and forth with the others, between the kitchen and reception, with plate after plate of the stuff. The room kept filling up, but we were so busy I didn't even know if there were any film stars in the crowd until there was a sudden lull, as someone introduced the mayor. It was during his speech welcoming Pocket Money Pictures to the city that Marcie hissed, "There he is, Joanne. Oh, doesn't he look gorgeous?"

"Who?" Joanne asked.

"Johnny Random, of course, There, at that table, surrounded by all the reporters."

I glanced in the direction that Marcie indicated. Johnny Random was sitting with a bored look on his face as he nibbled on one of the canapés.

"Oh look," Marcie said. "Get a load of that dress."

"I wonder what a dress like that costs. It looks like silk," Joanne said. "And would you look at the slit on the side. It goes almost to her hip. She's showing off more leg than I am with my mini. I bet she's one of the stars."

"You're right," I said. "That's Zulan Maisoneuve. She's the co-star."

"Her name sounds French, but she looks Chinese," Joanne said.

"She was born in Vietnam, actually, but her mother was Chinese and her father was French. But her real name is Michelle Tremblay."

"Okay. So tell us who's that old lady with the blue hair. I bet you don't know who that is," Joanne said.

I groaned. It was Aunt Phyllis.

"No, I haven't a clue who she is," I mumbled.

Just then I noticed that Celia had joined us and was giving me a quizzical look. I blushed.

There was some polite applause as the mayor finished his speech and Robert Rudsnicker was asked if he would say a few words on behalf of Pocket Money Pictures.

I didn't get a chance to hear much of what he said because Mr. Nicholson called us all into the kitchen to get ready to serve the hot food.

We scurried in and out of the kitchen for the next few minutes, putting the hot dishes of steaming food on the tables. Robert Rudsnicker's speech was short and I noticed he wasn't stammering too badly. I caught a glimpse of Aunt Phyllis sitting near the front. She seemed to be hanging on every word Robert Rudsnicker was saying and she had one hand poised in the air, as if she was in the middle of conducting an orchestra. I hoped I could get through the evening without bumping into her.

Robert Rudsnicker finished his short speech by introducing some of the actors and film crew, and then there was a mad rush for the food, led, it seemed, by the reporters.

We got a few minutes in the kitchen to gulp down some food ourselves, while Mr. Nicholson and Bruce supervised out in the reception hall.

"So, Celia," Joanne was saying between mouthfuls, "when we go out there again, I want you to point out the man most likely to get me into films. What about that Robert Rudsnicker guy?"

"He's the director," I said. "Someone else actually does the casting."

"Okay, Celia, point *him* out."

"Oh, knock it off, Joanne," Marcie said. "You're giving me a headache."

Mr. Nicholson rushed in with Bruce. "Okay everybody. Bruce and I are going to set up the crêpes out in the reception hall. I want all of you to come with me and Bruce. Grab one of those service carts. They're all ready. As soon as Bruce and I have made up some crêpes, put some on the carts and circulate among the guests. You all know how to do the flambé part. The brandy and Gran Marnier are on the cart, and there are toppings of whipped cream and fresh raspberries. Oh Harry, I forgot about you. You'd better keep an eye on things on the tables, make sure the sugar bowls and cream jugs are kept filled for the coffee and so on. If the crêpes prove popular, we'll press you into service somehow. Okay, everyone, let's go."

I followed the others out into the reception hall. Mr. Nicholson and Bruce had two stations set up and were soon busy cooking up batches of crêpes on small burners. I checked the tables and took sugar bowls and cream jugs back and forth, filling them as needed, and keeping one eye out for Aunt Phyllis. But I needn't have worried. In a far corner of the room Aunt Phyllis had somehow managed to surround herself with a mob of reporters. They were scribbling on their notepads like mad.

"We need you." It was Joanne. "Everyone and their dog wants these crêpes. They've eaten most of the prepared desserts already and they still want crêpes."

"What do I do?"

"I'll show you. Follow me. I'll do one and then you can have this cart and I'll get another from the kitchen."

I followed Joanne to a crowded table. "How many for crêpes flambé?" she asked. Three people raised their hands.

I watched as Joanne carefully lifted a crêpe onto a small plate, then poured a small amount of brandy onto it, followed by a dash of Gran Marnier. Then quickly taking a long match-like stick, she touched it to a flickering alcohol burner on the cart. She ignited the crêpe, which flamed with a blue flame. She placed the flaming crêpe in front of one of the people seated at the table and then helped him with the raspberries and cream. She served two more people at the table in the same way.

"Okay," she said. "Think you can do that?"

"I think so."

"Okay kiddo. You're on your own. Serve the next table. I'm off to get another cart to serve that guy over there. Celia tells me he's my best bet for being discovered. She said if anyone can get me into a part, it's him. His name is Ralph."

I would have laughed if I'd had time to think about it, but some people at the next table were waving me over to serve them crêpes.

I glanced at the small stack of crêpes on my cart which were being kept warm by a hot box underneath. "How many for crêpes?" I asked. Of the seven people sitting around the table, five shot up their hands. I was nervous. I was going to have to serve flaming crêpes with an audience watching every move. Well, here goes, I thought. I did want a chance to act, and here was a chance to make like I knew exactly what I was doing. The people at the table were obviously reporters, as most of them were holding cameras and notepads. I glanced at the pile of crêpes that were left on my cart and knew I'd have to get some more. I scooped up the first crêpe and followed the steps that Joanne had shown me. I was a lot slower, but everything worked out okay and I was quite pleased with myself when I set the first flaming crêpe in front of a reporter. Then I noticed that one of the people sitting at the table was Johnny Random.

"Hey kid, give us a shot of that brandy." I think he'd already been drinking, as his voice sounded slurred.

I was in the middle of lighting my third crêpe but the two reporters who'd already been served were reaching onto the cart to help themselves to the toppings. I served the third crêpe when Johnny Random said, "Hey, kid, where's mine?"

I hadn't noticed that he'd raised his hand earlier, but I had one crêpe left.

"How about some raspberries?" a reporter asked.

I was getting a bit flustered what with trying to hand out the toppings, serving the crêpe, and getting it lit. Nothing happened when I touched the flaming sliver of wood to the crêpe. I guess I'd taken too long to light it and some of the brandy had evaporated. I added a bit more and was preparing to try again, when Johnny Random grabbed the brandy bottle and took a large swig. I'd just got the crêpe lit, and was placing it in front of him, when he brought the bottle down onto the table with a thump. More brandy splashed onto the burning crêpe. There was a huge *whoomp!* A flame about two feet high leaped up from the crêpe just as Johnny Random leaned over it.

He gasped and reared back in fright. Unfortunately he hadn't swallowed the mouthful of brandy that he'd swigged from the bottle and he spewed it across the table over the flaming crêpe, and another long flame shot across the tablecloth. It was like a flame-thrower in one of those war movies. The reporters, who had already leaped to their feet when the first flame went up, now jumped backwards. Johnny Random had already reared back to escape the flames but he must have pushed hard against the table. His chair, with him still sitting in it, toppled back with a crash, but not before a series of flashes went off. I was dazed and thought there were more fires breaking out, but then I realized a few of the reporters had recovered enough to catch the whole thing on film.

The flames died quickly, leaving a large scorch mark across the white tablecloth. Then Celia was there. "Go," she hissed. "I'll take over. Go check on the coffee or something."

I hesitated, but not for long. She gave me a push. I found the table with the coffee pots and pretended to check them. Out of the corner of my eye I saw someone help Johnny Random out of the room, as the cameras went on flashing. There was a sudden lack of interest in crêpes flambé and the reception seemed to be breaking up.

I was still shaken up by what had happened and I could feel my heart pounding in my chest. I tried to look busy, rearranging the coffee cups on the table, and I didn't notice, until too late, that Aunt Phyllis and Robert Rudsnicker were right beside me, helping themselves to coffee.

Aunt Phyllis was saying, "There I was, right in the middle of telling the reporters about one of my roles in theatre, when Johnny Random caused that commotion. He is such a publicity hound. Before I knew it, I was sitting there talking to myself. He's so inconsiderate. Always seeking the limelight."

There was no escape. I held my breath, waiting for Aunt Phyllis to notice me and introduce me to Robert Rudsnicker as her nephew. I'd had enough embarrassment for one night. But I was in luck. Aunt Phyllis was so engrossed in her conversation she moved off without so much as a glance in my direction. But I saw Robert Rudsnicker glance at me and, by the look on his face, I could tell he was wondering where he'd seen me before.

* * *

We were all assembled in the kitchen.

"I don't know what happened," Mr. Nicholson was saying, "or how Harry got involved. He hasn't any experience with burning alcohol. Well, for now let's tidy up and hope we don't get sued. Joanne, I need to talk to you. That section was your service area. The rest of you get packed up and put everything in the vans."

We scampered off, leaving Joanne with Mr. Nicholson in the kitchen. I felt terrible, but it wasn't all my fault. I wanted to explain, but it didn't seem to be the right time. I was thankful that Mr. Nicholson was taking it so calmly and Chef Antonio wasn't in charge.

Bruce was going to drive us home. I was the last to get in the van. Marcie and Dawn were laughing.

"I told Mr. Nicholson that I just got too busy and needed help," Joanne was saying. "I said I didn't know Harry here wasn't experienced and would set an actor on fire. After all, I did hear Henry say that if we got busy, we'd use Harry. I think Henry bought it. He's a real sweetheart. So Harry, make sure you cover for me, okay, and none of us will get fired. But I may not be here long myself. I got a date with that casting guy you pointed out to me, Celia. He invited me to meet him at his room in The Ritz. He said he'd give me an audition. Maybe I'll be a star." Joanne laughed hysterically and the others joined in. I glanced back at Celia, who seemed about to say something, but she closed her mouth and looked out the window.

We came to our stop and I got out with Celia. Joanne, Dawn, and Marcie were still laughing.

I was too embarrassed to say anything to Celia as I walked beside her. I was still going over what had happened in my head and I was surprised when she stopped outside a house just a half block down the street.

"See you tomorrow, Harry, okay? At the bus stop on the corner at nine?"

"You think I'll be allowed on the set after what happened?"

"Don't worry. We're not likely to run into Johnny Random. They don't start shooting until late next week and nobody else will know who you are. I've already got the pass. Anyway, it was really my fault. Joanne kept bugging me all night to point out someone who would get her into the movies. She just wouldn't let up. So I pointed out Ralph and told a little white lie. I did it as a joke to get her off my back. I'd no idea she would stick you with her job. I was going to tell her the truth about Ralph, but what the heck. She can look after herself."

I guess I still looked worried because, before she went up the sidewalk to her house, she squeezed my arm and said, "Don't worry. It'll work out. You'll see."

12

"ROBERT GAVE A LOVELY speech last night," Aunt Phyllis was saying. "Hardly a stammer. My breathing exercises worked wonderfully. But that Johnny Random made a fool of himself."

Dad looked up from reading the sports page of the *Morning Independent*. "Oh, what did he do?"

"I'm not sure. Caused some kind of commotion. Set fire to the tablecloth or something. He's so immature. That young man was too successful too soon and it's gone to his head. He'll burn himself out before long."

Dad laughed. "I thought he only burned the tablecloth. Sounds like our Harry."

I got really interested in spreading jam on my toast, as Aunt Phyllis gave Dad a withering look. Before I'd left for school yesterday, I'd told Mom I'd be working late at The Ritz. At that time I didn't know anything about the reception and I wasn't about to enlighten them now.

"Robert is beside himself with worry that the film will be a flop with Johnny Random in the leading role," Aunt Phyllis continued.

"So," Dad asked, "have you found out what your part is? Maybe you can save the film, win an Oscar."

"Well, as a matter of fact, Robert told me last night that I'll be playing a rich Chinese dowager, one of the nobility, mother of the ruler of the province, I believe. It's only a small part and I've only got a few lines, but it's important and rather exciting. At one point, I believe I'm being transported through the streets in the middle of a rabble of peasants who are rioting."

"Sounds like type-casting to me." Dad chuckled. "You riding in a taxi when everyone else has to walk."

"Actually, I believe it's a sedan chair or a rickshaw. It was before the time of automobiles in China."

"Well, you should fit right in then, if it was the Ming Dynasty."

"George!" This time it was Mom who gave Dad a look that said "don't be insulting."

Dad went back to reading his paper. Dad always reads the sports page first and I glanced at the front section that he'd dropped to the floor. I stifled a gasp.

There was a large photo right on the front page with the caption "Film Star Flambéed." The rest of the caption, in smaller print, read "Well-known film star, Johnny Random, looked like a fire-eater when he got too close to a crêpe Suzette at a reception at city hall last night. More on page 5." In the photo, a really freaked-out Johnny Random had a flame shooting from his mouth across the table. Opposite him were a couple of startled faces, and at the left hand edge of the photo, there I was. Although you could only see the back of my bald head, I was obviously the waiter in the white jacket.

I swallowed the last of my toast and stumbled to my feet. I had to get out of there before Dad or anyone else saw the front page.

"Gotta go," I mumbled at Mom's inquiring look.

I wasted no time getting out of the house but, before I left, I grabbed an old cap from the hall closet. I was sure everyone who saw my bald head would recognize it, and me, as the guy who tried to fry Johnny Random. Maybe I should forget about meeting Celia. I was sure my photo would be plastered over the gates to the film set like a *Wanted Dead or Alive* poster with a caption, "Under No Circumstances Is This Person to Be Permitted On This Property."

I walked around a couple of blocks to kill time. I was early. I couldn't very well not show up. What would Celia think?

At five minutes to nine I strolled to the bus stop. Celia was already there.

"Hi." She smiled. "Why the cap?"

"Disguise," I said, keeping my voice down so the other three people waiting for the bus wouldn't hear. One of them had just put some money in the newspaper box that sold the *Morning Independent* and was scanning the front page. "Have you seen the newspaper?" I nodded towards the newspaper box.

"No." Celia walked to the box and stared through the plastic front. She fumbled in her pocket for some change and bought one of the papers just as the bus pulled up. She was smiling as we boarded the bus.

There weren't many people on the bus and we found a seat to ourselves. Celia had the newspaper on her lap and was examining the photo.

"You can't really tell it's you." She grinned. "It could be anyone. You can only see the back of your head."

"Well, it isn't very hard to figure out," I said. "That reception was catered by The Ritz and I'm the only high school kid with a bald head who works for The Ritz."

"You can't tell from this photo that you're a high school student. You could be an old man." Celia laughed. "Let's see what it says on page five." She opened the newspaper and we both read silently for a minute. "It's just reporting what the mayor and Robert Rudsnicker said," Celia said. "Nothing to worry about."

"No. That's the wrong bit. Look what it says here." I pointed to another piece on the same page that had "continued from page 1" on it. The words seemed to jump from the page. "Oscar-winning star Johnny Random, here to star in *Funeral at Feng-t'ai*, had a narrow escape last night at a civic reception in city hall to welcome Pocket Money Pictures. During the serving of crêpes Suzette, which are served flambéed, some alcohol caught fire right in front of where the star was sitting. No injuries were reported, but the actor was apparently lucky. The mayor said the incident was unfortunate and he had no idea what had gone wrong. When contacted late last night, a spokesperson for The Ritz Hotel, which catered the event, declined comment, except to say that the incident will be investigated. Johnny Random was also unavailable for comment."

I groaned. "I can't wait until Monday. An investigation."

"Oh dear," Celia said. "I'm sorry. But you should never have been put in that situation. You wouldn't have been, if I hadn't told Joanne to go talk to Ralph. Tell me what happened, anyway."

I told her the whole story, about how Johnny Random seemed to be drunk and grabbed the bottle of brandy.

"So it was his own fault," Celia said. "I heard he was a bit of a jerk and has been giving room service a rough time. If you get asked, just tell them what happened."

"Who'll believe me? It's my word against the great Johnny Random. And then there's my reputation. You know what they call me?"

"You mean Harry *Flammable*? I wondered about that. So tell me."

I did — all the crazy incidents that had happened to earn me my nickname. Celia was in stitches, laughing.

"Except for maybe the grass fire incident, none of them were your fault. Well, I guess you did light the Bunsen burner in science class. But you've just been unlucky."

"Yeah, but how unlucky can you get? Well, at least I won't have to go on pretending I'm enjoying working at The Ritz. But I guess it's too late to find another job. I'll just lose the credits, which means I'll have to make them up next term, when I should really be finished school."

"Oh, don't be such a pessimist. A few weeks from now you'll look back on what's happened and think the whole thing was hilarious. Think of it as part of life's experience. It'll make you a better person."

"How?"

"I dunno. I don't have all the answers. Look, we're almost at the film set. I was looking forward to showing you around, but it won't be much fun if you're going to mope about things. What's happened, happened, and you can't do anything about it. So do you want to come or not?"

"Yeah. Sorry. I didn't mean to spoil your day. You're right. I can't do anything about it."

"And if you let your hair grow back, in a few weeks nobody will recognize you anyway." Celia chuckled. "So why did you cut it off?"

"I just got tired of everyone telling me to get a haircut," I said.

"You're funny." Celia laughed.

The bus slowed and made a wide U-turn. It was the end of the run. We were out in the country and the only ones left on the bus.

We climbed off and Celia led the way up a gravel road that led through a security fence with a hut just inside the gate. A traffic barrier was closed across the road. A sign on the fence read POCKET MONEY PICTURES.

"Oh here. Pin this on." Celia pulled a small laminated card from her pocket that said "Visitors Pass — Pocket Money Pictures." When she helped me pin it on my jacket she looked into my eyes and smiled. We hadn't been this close before and I took a second to stare back at her. She caught me staring and blushed slightly.

"Come on. Follow me." She walked through the gate and around the traffic barrier, with me close on her heels. She stuck her head in the open window of the hut and showed her pass, then indicated me. "He's my guest. He's got a visitor's pass."

The security guard waved us on and called "Have a good day."

I breathed a sigh of relief. There was no one looking out for my face, to order me thrown off the premises.

"The set is over this hill and down in a valley," Celia said, "but, if we walk to the top of the bigger hill on our left, you can see the whole thing laid out below and it'll give you a better idea of how the whole scene looks. Then we'll walk down into it. They're hoping to start shooting next week. Robert Rudsnicker comes here every morning, then spends the afternoon at The Ritz. I think he's still making changes to the script."

We left the road and scrambled up the steep, grassy hill.

"Wow!" I gasped. "It's fantastic."

Below, in a large compound behind a high wall, a large castle-like structure dominated an ancient Chinese street. Workers carrying ladders and tools moved about, and there was a sound of hammering and power-saws. A building, with a tiled roof that curved upward at the ends, stood at one end of the street and a tall pagoda rose behind it in the distance. Beyond the castle there was a shimmering blue sea.

"The sea! It looks real! Look at the way it sparkles."

"That's my tinfoil," Celia said. "I must admit it looks really good from here. Up close though, it looks really phony. All the building fronts are made of plywood, painted to look old. Look, they're still painting one of the walls of the castle. It looks like stone and it's all rough and bumpy because it has to be climbed. That building at the end, with the curved roof and the pagoda behind it, is supposed to be a temple."

"There's a railway line running down the edge of the street." I pointed.

"Yeah," Celia said. "They have a train that's gonna be part of the action. Look over there." She pointed across a small valley where a long wooden trestle bridge spanned a high ravine. Workers were swarming over it, painting the timbers to give the bridge a weathered look.

"So where's the train?" I asked.

"It's parked behind the hill on the far side of the trestle. It's an old steam engine. It's really neat. Want to go see it?"

"Sure," I said. "This is fantastic."

We crossed the valley, rounded the hill, and climbed to the rail line. There, a huge, really old-fashioned-looking steam engine, hooked to three equally old, green passenger cars, stood on a length of rail a short distance from the bridge.

"Does it run?" I asked.

"Yes. It's really a diesel engine, but it used to be a real steam engine. They've changed it to make it look older, and it can produce smoke and steam somehow, like the real thing."

"So what's supposed to happen?" I asked. "What's the action?"

"It's a peasant uprising. They're starving and being oppressed by the Chinese nobility. The peasants attack the castle and some of them take over the train and drive it into the town and help in the attack. Your friend Johnny Random is supposed to be the leader of the peasants. The title is from an early scene in the movie. When the hero is a child, his father dies. During the funeral procession, the Chinese ruler of the province and his bodyguards virtually trample the mourners into the mud and the child's mother is knocked down. He never forgets this cruelty.

"His girlfriend, played by Zulan Maisoneuve — she was at the reception too — is being held in the castle by the same Chinese lord, who wants to keep the peasants in slavery. Zulan, or Li Ching, as she's called in the movie, and Johnny Random, I forget his Chinese name, are long-time childhood sweethearts and Li Ching is grabbed by the ruler to be one of his concubines, but ends up as a hostage.

"Paul Tinyan is playing the Chinese ruler. He hasn't arrived yet. I think he gets here next week, but most of his part will be filmed in China.

"Anyway, Johnny Random and his rebels are not only fighting for more rice or better government or something, but they also want to rescue Li Ching."

"It sounds great. They'll need lots of extras. When are they getting the extras for the battle scene?"

"They did already in March sometime. During spring break. I wasn't here then. You didn't try out? I think it was in the newspapers."

"We were away at spring break, visiting Mom's sister. I didn't know anything about it then. I was counting on getting on with Pocket Money Pictures with the work experience program."

"Sorry about that," Celia said. "I put my name in because I was already with The Ritz and I wanted something different. But I heard you had to look Asian for a part as an extra."

"Johnny Random doesn't look Asian," I said.

"No, but it's easier for the make up department to make one guy look Asian than a couple of hundred extras. Come on. Let's go down into the street."

We ran down the hill and walked along the edge of the street beside the railway line. All around us workers were putting the finishing touches to the building fronts. A water truck drove along the street, wetting it down to keep down the dust.

"In the movie," Celia said, "I think they are going to have this street all muddy."

"Why do they have a switch in the railway line here?" I asked.

"Oh, they had a little branch line and they used the engine to haul some of the construction material when they were building the castle. But now that it's finished, they tore it up. Come on, I'll show you my tinfoil sea."

We walked down a narrow alley beside the castle. At the back, running the length of most of the street, was a curved billboard-like structure, painted different shades of blue. Dangling from the billboard, at various heights, were hundreds of pieces of tinfoil.

I gaped. "You hung all these?"

"Yeah, and I'm nearly finished. I just have to do a little bit at the far end."

We walked to the end where a small, adjustable, elevated platform with wheels was parked. I followed Celia onto the platform and she pushed a control button. It rose slowly and stopped when Celia pressed the button again. "It works on hydraulics," she said.

A large container of tinfoil sat on one corner of the platform along with a large spool of clear fishing line.

"It doesn't look very real when you're right up against it," Celia said. "Here's what I have to do." She took a sheet of tinfoil and cut off a strip. Then she snipped off a length of fishing line and attached it to the tinfoil with a small hook. She picked up a large stapler and stapled the piece of line to the billboard.

"It has to hang free, so it can move to give the impression of sunlight on water. Here, you try one. Then at least you can say you had a part in making the movie." She laughed.

I had just completed stapling my piece of line with its tinfoil when we heard voices and laughter right behind us.

The voices were coming from behind the plywood wall of the castle. We weren't high enough to see over the wall and whoever was on the other side was too close to the wall to see us.

"Did you hear what happened to Johnny Random?" a voice asked.

"That's Ralph," Celia whispered.

"He almost went up in flames at the reception last night when some kid served him a flaming crêpe. Of course, he was drunk."

"Who? The waiter?" a second voice asked.

"No, Johnny Random. You know how he drinks. He was belting back a brandy and I hear it caught fire. Well, the *Funeral at Feng-t'ai* was almost Johnny's." Ralph laughed.

"Well, whoever that poor kid was that served him, it'll probably be his funeral when Johnny sobers up," the other voice replied.

"That Johnny Random is really arrogant. You know, he was complaining the other day the lighting in his trailer wasn't bright enough, so I had to change all the bulbs. As far as I'm concerned, if I meet that kid I'd like to shake his hand."

"I don't think you'd want to do that," Celia whispered to me.

Ralph was laughing. "I hear makeup will probably have to give Johnny a new set of eyebrows. I suppose he'll want the lighting in his trailer darker now."

"I'll bet that kid got fired," the second voice said.

"You know, that girl, Celia, was working at the reception," Ralph continued. "She'll know what happened. She should be here soon."

"I think I'd better go," I whispered.

"Yeah, I guess so," Celia said. "I don't think it's a good idea to be here right now. Ralph might recognize you and he'll only ask awkward questions. Anyway, it's time for me to start work."

"Thanks for showing me around," I whispered. "See you Monday." I jumped lightly to the ground and hurried along the back of the castle wall. Before I turned into the alley I looked back to wave, but thought better of it. Ralph was standing at the foot of the platform, talking to Celia.

As I rode back to the city, I thought, *why did I say, "See you Monday" to Celia*? Tomorrow was Sunday. I should have asked if I could see her then. I had all of Sunday to get through before I faced the music on Monday. Being with Celia tomorrow would have made facing Monday a bit more bearable. But I'd blown it.

13

I WAS SURE BY the time I got home everyone would have seen the newspaper and I would have to face a barrage of questions.

Aunt Phyllis was vacuuming the living room rug and Mom was cleaning the windows. Dad was nowhere in sight.

"We had lunch about a half hour ago," Mom said. "There's some soup left in the fridge. You can heat it up in the microwave."

"Um. No thanks. Is there any of that pizza left?"

"I think there's a couple of slices."

I heated the pizza and was just sitting down to eat it when Dad came in from the backyard.

"Where's the newspaper?" Dad asked.

Uh oh, I thought. Here it comes. The inquisition. Like, "When you said you wanted to be in pictures, did you mean the front page of the *Morning Independent*?"

"I haven't seen it," Mom said.

Aunt Phyllis was putting the vacuum cleaner away. "What are you looking for, George?"

"The newspaper. I need the sports page. There's a wrestling card tonight at the stadium and I'm thinking of going. I want to check who the headliners are."

"Wrestling indeed, how uncultured," Aunt Phyllis said. "Well, I'm sorry George, I thought you were finished with it. I was helping to tidy up. You left it on the floor and I put it in the recycling box at the end of the hall. By the way, I also put that green plastic lizard that you left on the end of my bed into the plastic recycling box. I thought that joke had been rather overworked."

"Not me this time," Dad said.

I was already halfway down the hall when I heard Mom say, "Oh dear, I put the boxes out at the end of the driveway."

I did a U-turn and dashed out the front door to the driveway. The blue boxes were there, but they were both empty.

I'd no idea how long ago the boxes had been emptied, but I knew I had to get to the recycling depot fast to have any chance of preventing Ralph from becoming part of a compacted bundle of plastic. The trouble was, the recycling depot was halfway across town. I raced into the garage and grabbed my bicycle. I hadn't ridden it for a couple of years and I'd been getting too big for it then. I jumped on, then jumped off just as fast. Both tires were flat. I found the pump and frantically pumped air into each tire, jumped on the bike again, and pedalled like mad. My bike seemed to have shrunk since I'd last ridden it. The seat was too low and it felt like my knees were up around my ears. But I thought about Ralph and tried to pedal faster.

I knew it was really my fault. I'd been in such a rush to get out of the house this morning I'd forgotten to put Ralph in his aquarium. He'd spent the night in the little grapefruit tree that I'd grown from seed in third grade. I often let him out in the tree and he usually stayed there. This time he hadn't, and I must have left my bedroom door open.

It took me a good half hour to reach the recycling depot. I flew into the yard, flung my bike against the fence, and dashed inside the building.

I was sweating and breathing hard. A forklift lumbered past carrying a large compacted bundle of cardboard. Another man at the far end of the building was operating the compactor.

I ran up to him. "Where's …" I tried to catch my breath. "Where's the plastic you brought in today?"

"Why? You lose something?"

"My aunt …" I was still panting.

"Your aunt?" The man laughed. "You trying to recycle your aunt?"

"No. It's my iguana." I'd finally got my breath back. "My aunt put him in the plastic recycling by mistake."

"An iguana. That's a lizard, right? Well, all the plastic we brought in today is still outside. There'll be another truck coming in before we close. I'll show you where the plastic is and you're welcome to look through it. I guess your aunt doesn't like lizards."

I wasn't going to explain. It was too complicated and I wanted to save what energy I had left for the search.

"Here it is. Good luck."

I groaned. Three huge steel mesh bins were jammed with plastic bottles and containers of every description.

"Oh, if you take the plastic containers out, make sure you put them back before you leave, okay?"

I nodded and set to work. It took me over an hour to get through the first bin. I had to haul out every bottle and I had to peer inside those that had an opening large enough for Ralph to crawl into. I'd just got the first bin loaded again when a truck drove in and reversed towards an empty bin.

I ran up to the driver's window and explained what I was looking for. If I could get the plastic dumped on the ground, I could sort it faster. The driver and his helper said they hadn't seen any lizards but they'd do what I asked, as long as I promised to fill the container as I went through the pile.

I was about halfway through the pile when a voice called, "Hey Harry! Did ya get a new job?"

I looked up to see Joe Straka peering at me through the fence. The auto wreckers was next to the recycling depot. He was holding some car part in his hand.

"I'm looking for Ralph," I explained. "Aunt Phyllis tried to recycle him. She thought he was made of plastic. What are you doing here on a Saturday?"

"Just earning a few extra bucks. Let me give you a hand. It'll go faster with two of us looking." Joe dropped the part on the ground, clambered over the fence, and helped me search.

We finished the pile and loaded the last of it into the bin. There was no sign of Ralph, but there were two more bins to search.

"He could be anywhere," Joe said. "Even if he was in the plastic, he could have taken off by now."

"Yeah. But there's still a chance he's still here."

"Did you see that picture on the front of the *Morning Independent*? It sure looked like you. That's why I asked if you'd got a new job. Did you see it? But I figured it couldn't have been you. It was at city hall, not at The Ritz, so it couldn't have been you."

"It was me." I told Joe the whole story. "I can't wait 'till Monday. Everyone will have seen the picture."

"Well, I wasn't sure it was you," Joe said. "Just deny it."

"If you'd read the rest of the paper you'd have seen that The Ritz was doing the catering. By Monday it won't take a genius to figure out it was me. And then I have to go to The Ritz in the afternoon. That's when I'll get fired."

"Still, it wasn't your fault," Joe sympathized. "It's not fair."

"Hey Joe!" a voice yelled. "Where are ya hidin'?"

"That's my boss," Joe said. "I'd better get back. Mr. Shamberg will have a fit if there are two firings from the work experience program in one weekend." He clambered back over the fence.

"Thanks for the help, Joe."

"Hey Joe!" the voice called again.

"Coming, Mr. Hardacre," Joe called. He waved at me, grabbed up the car part from the ground, and disappeared behind a row of wrecked cars.

I'd just got the last bin finished when the guy I'd talked to came up. "Any luck?"

I shook my head.

"Look, we're closing up. Why don't you give me your name and phone number and I'll call you if it shows up."

"Okay. Thanks." I described what Ralph looked like and, before I left, I made a quick check along the fence and the yard, but as Joe said, Ralph could be anywhere by now.

It was just about dark when I got home. I jumped off my bike at the end of the driveway and was wheeling it towards the garage when a slight movement caught my eye. It came from the small tree at the edge of the lawn. It was Ralph.

"Darn you! Do you know how many bleach and milk containers I looked in today?" I could have been mad at Ralph but I was too relieved that he was still alive.

Dad had gone to the wrestling and Aunt Phyllis had gone to bed. Mom was pleased that I'd found Ralph. By the time I'd wolfed down supper, I was nodding off. I was exhausted. I went to bed, but before I did I made sure that Ralph was safely in his aquarium.

When I woke up and looked at the clock, I saw that I'd slept in. I thought, *that's good. If Sunday goes by fast, the waiting for Monday won't be so bad. But, then, on the other hand, I don't want Monday to come at all. Still, I have to get through this day.*

I got dressed and went to the kitchen. Through the window I could see Dad in the back garden. There was no sign of Mom or Aunt Phyllis.

I heated up a couple of waffles in the toaster and was just sitting down to eat them when Dad came in.

"Oh hi, Harry. Mom said you found Ralph. I'm glad. Is he okay?"

"Yeah, he was in the tree at the edge of the lawn. I'd left him in the tree in my bedroom yesterday and forgot to close my bedroom door."

"Well, I guess he must have played dead or something when Aunt Phyllis picked him up." Dad laughed.

"Where are Mom and Aunt Phyllis?" I asked.

"Your mom is practising for some concert in the community hall. Aunt Phyllis went along with her, no doubt to give your mother advice on her singing career. I offered to take Aunt Phyllis to the wrestling last night, but she said it would only disgust her. She should have come." Dad laughed. "Some of those wrestlers could have done with some acting tips. They were pathetic. Well, I'd better get some more done outside. I'm fixing up the greenhouse. You can give me a hand, if you like, when you finish your breakfast. See ya later."

I finished my waffles and thought about phoning Celia. I wasn't sure what I'd say, but it was getting on my nerves, just sitting around and waiting, not knowing what was going to happen tomorrow. We could at least talk. I looked up the number in the phone book and dialed, but there was nobody home. I decided to help Dad with the greenhouse. At least it would kill some time.

Dad and I had just come in from outside and were having some lunch when the front door burst open. Both of us leaped to our feet at the sight of Mom and Aunt Phyllis. At first glance it looked like they'd been attacked by an axe murderer. From head to toe they were covered in some kind of red splatter and I thought for a minute that Mom had some brain matter in her hair.

Dad gasped. "What happened? Was your singing so bad that they threw food?"

I was standing there, gaping, when Dad's words sunk in. Aunt Phyllis scurried downstairs, looking mortified.

Mom went and stood in front of the small mirror near the sink and examined her head. "Don't ask," she said. "Oh lord." She began picking what I thought was the brain matter out of her hair.

"What's that stuff?" I asked.

"Spaghetti."

"Spaghetti?" Dad and I chorused.

"Yeah, spaghetti." Then Mom burst out laughing as she looked at herself in the mirror.

"But what happened?" I asked.

Mom was now laughing so hard she had trouble getting the words out but it sounded like she said, "Aunt Phyllis said I needed more resonance."

"Resonance? Is that some kind of spaghetti sauce?" I asked.

"No, Harry." Mom giggled and then burst into gales of laughter. "It's an echo effect. I'd been singing 'Indian Love Call' from *Rose-Marie*. You know the song. It goes, 'when I'm calling you …'" Mom sang a few bars. "After practice …" Mom's laughter threatened to get out of control again. "After practice we were walking along the alley behind the community hall. Aunt Phyllis was going on about the need to have my voice vibrate more when she spotted this dumpster." Mom howled.

"Dumpster?" Dad asked.

Mom got a bit more control back. "Yeah. Oh dear. She got me to sing into the dumpster."

"Yuck!" I said.

"Actually, it was quite clean, almost new and practically empty." Mom was wiping tears of laughter from her eyes. "Anyway, Aunt Phyllis suggested that our community hall needed some kind of sound well in front of the stage and that we might even use the dumpster. She suggested I climb up on it and try singing into it …" Mom started to break up again. "There I was, standing on top of the dumpster, singing into it, and …" Mom snorted with laughter and almost choked. "And I fell in." Now Mom really let loose and Dad and I had to wait quite a while before she recovered enough to continue.

She was still snickering but we could follow what she was saying. "Aunt Phyllis climbed up on the dumpster too and grabbed my hand and was trying to pull me up … and …" Mom almost exploded again but raced on. "She fell in too." Mom collapsed with laughter on top of the sink and again Dad and I had to wait for her to recover.

"We landed on a couple of soft garbage bags but, before we could move, someone came and dumped a huge load of leftover spaghetti and sauce on us. We shrieked, I can tell you, when the spaghetti hit us. It turned out that the dumpster is owned by a new Italian restaurant that had just opened. The poor kid who'd dumped the spaghetti on us got the scare of his life. He must have heard us shriek, but when he saw us scrambling out, he ran like mad to the restaurant. Probably to get an ambulance or something. We got out of there quick before anyone showed up, and practically ran the whole way home. It was hilarious!" Mom laughed some more but she'd got most of the laughter out of her system by now. "I'd better go and clean up. Oh, I've changed my mind about what we're having for supper." She burst out laughing again as she disappeared into the bathroom. "It was going to be spaghetti." Her laughter echoed from inside the bathroom.

That episode helped take my mind off things for a while. Dad and I kept picturing the scene in our minds and had laughing fits of our own.

Before I went to bed I got the dictionary and looked up the word Mom had used. "Resonance: the quality or condition of being resonant." Not very helpful. Then, "the enhancement of the response of an electrical or mechanical system to a periodic driving force …" I skipped the rest of that. Further down I found, "strong and deep in tone; resounding; a resonant voice." That had to be it. Then I saw, "continuing to sound in the ears or memory." That last bit, unfortunately, reminded me of what might be in store for me tomorrow. Once the incident at city hall reached all the ears at school, I wouldn't be allowed to forget it.

14

WHEN I WALKED INTO class there were hoots of laughter and someone yelled, "Way to go, Harry!" I'd been right about it not taking a genius to figure out it was me in the picture in the *Morning Independent.* Somebody had made three photocopies of it, enlarged about three sizes, and stuck them to the chalkboard. Cartoon word balloons were drawn in chalk around the edges. In one I was saying, "You say there was a *firefly* in the soup, sir?" In another, the flame-throwing Johnny Random was saying, "What do you have to do to get a lousy glass of water in this dump?" and the third one had me saying "Will that be cash or cremation?"

Joe Straka came up and clapped me on the shoulder. "Stay cool, man."

I put on a brave face but I wasn't feeling cool. It didn't help when the last announcement on the P.A. for the morning was, "Would Harry Flam-uh-Flanagan please go to Mr. Shamberg's office now please."

Well, I thought as I walked down the hall, *I guess this is it. Maybe I won't have to show up at The Ritz after all.* It would be a relief if Mr. Shamberg told me I'd been fired.

Mr. Shamberg's door was open and he was sitting behind his desk. "Come in, Harry. Have a seat."

I sat as Mr. Shamberg shuffled through some papers. The orangutan poster with its "hang in there baby" caption didn't offer me much comfort. Instead the nursery rhyme "Rockabye Baby" started running through my head. I wasn't sure if I was the baby in the cradle or I was underneath the tree, but I knew the bough was about to come crashing down.

Mr. Shamberg stopped shuffling through the papers and looked up. "Harry, I can't find your work experience employment activity sheet. Did you turn it in?"

"My employment activity sheet," I repeated. I wondered what was the use of it now. "I got it signed and …" What had I done with it? I remembered taking it home on Thursday and I knew I had it with me when I'd got to school on Friday. I had it in my pants pocket. I groaned. It was still in my pocket. The pocket of the pants I'd changed out of and left at The Ritz Friday night before going to the reception.

"Sorry, Mr. Shamberg. I had it on Friday morning, but I forgot to turn it in. It's in my other pair of pants at The Ritz."

"Okay. Make sure you pick it up today and turn it in to me tomorrow."

I sat there.

"That's all," Mr. Shamberg said. "You can go."

That's all. I couldn't believe it. No mention of what had happened at the reception. No mention about an irate phone call from The Ritz. If all the kids in my class knew about the reception incident, why didn't Mr. Shamberg? Should I mention what had happened and get it over with or wait until The Ritz actually fired me?

Mr. Shamberg looked puzzled. "I said that's all, Harry."

I came to a quick decision. I'd have to tell Mr. Shamberg when I got fired anyway. There was no point in going over what had happened twice. This was a reprieve. "Thanks," I mumbled and I scurried out of his office.

* * *

I was in the locker room at The Ritz, about to change into my uniform, when Kin came in.

"Oh, Harry, I have a message. Ms. Capstone in personnel office wants to see you. Maybe you get raise."

I could never tell if Kin was trying to be funny or what.

This time there was going to be no reprieve like in Mr. Shamberg's office this morning.

Again I had to wait in the outer office. The wait seemed longer this time. Finally the secretary ushered me into Ms. Capstone's office.

Ms. Capstone's eyebrows did their thing, which meant "take a seat." I did and waited some more. Her suit, this time, was red, and the belt she wore was black. For some reason, karate came to mind. Ms. Capstone was peering at a newspaper. Five or six more littered her desk and I could see that parts of them were highlighted in red. One of the newspapers was the *Morning Independent*, with the now infamous picture on the front page.

Ms. Capstone's hair was pinned back on both sides of her face and, as I waited nervously, I could see both eyebrows dancing like live, hairy caterpillars on her forehead as she scanned one of the newspapers. I noticed it was the *Globe Tribune*. I gulped. Surely I wasn't featured in newspapers all across the country. The *Morning Independent* was bad enough, but the *Globe Tribune* was a national morning newspaper.

Ms. Capstone closed the newspaper and looked at me. The way her eyebrows sprang together and then leaped apart, I think it was the first time she'd noticed I was bald.

"What happened to your hair?" her voice boomed. "It didn't catch fire too, did it?"

"Um, no. I shaved it off."

"Hmm. Well. You probably know why you're here." Ms. Capstone indicated the newspapers.

I nodded.

"When I interviewed you, I reminded you that The Ritz has a very high reputation and nothing should be allowed to sully that reputation. I said that the comfort and needs of our guests come first. Here, at The Ritz, we pride ourselves on privacy. We do not like our guests exposed to the prying eyes of reporters or gossip columnists. It seems, however, that you have single-handedly given The Ritz the publicity we do our best to avoid, and, I might add, in almost every major newspaper in the country.

"I must admit that my first instinct was to phone up your teacher, Mr. Shamrock, and tell him you were fired. Usually my first instinct is correct."

I didn't dare correct Ms. Capstone on Mr. Shamberg's name.

"However," Ms. Capstone went on, as her eyebrows seemed to be trying to circle her forehead, "on investigating this unfortunate incident, Mr. Henry Nicholson, in charge of our outside catering, spoke up on your behalf. Mr. Nicholson has a soft heart, but I respect his judgment. It appears you were pressed into service by a more experienced member of the team who was, it turns out, more interested in seeking a movie career than serving the guests of The Ritz. She tendered her resignation this morning to follow what she called an *acting career*. Your immediate supervisor in the kitchen, Kin Woo, also gave you a good reference.

"These people speaking on your behalf did not sway me, however, as it is my duty in public relations to make sure that none of The Ritz's employees do anything to smear the reputation of the hotel. What did sway me towards giving you one more chance was the column in the *Globe Tribune* by the columnist Marius Lippencott. You may have heard of him. He's a very respected journalist and I know him personally. He's stayed here on many occasions.

"Anyway, after reading his column, I telephoned him. He was an eyewitness to the fiasco, and from reading his column and what he said to me on the telephone, it appears that Mr. Random was the cause of his own misfortune. It would also appear that The Ritz is not about to be sued. We could have been, but we have also received a written apology from Mr. Robert Rudsnicker on behalf of Pocket Money Pictures for Mr. Random's behaviour. It appears also that Mr. Random has not been one of our most civil guests. Um, forget I said that. Confidentiality is paramount when dealing with our guests, no matter what the provocation. At The Ritz we must always endeavour to cater to our guests, no matter how difficult that may be at times.

"I am, therefore, giving you one more chance. I'm not sure it's the right decision but I am hopeful you will not get yourself in another situation that will discredit the good name of this hotel." Ms. Capstone's eyebrows stopped dancing and rested as though they had finished conducting an orchestra. "You may go."

"Thank you," I blurted as I rose to leave.

"Don't thank me. Thank Marius Lippencott."

I felt overjoyed. I wasn't fired. I changed quickly and went into the kitchen. Kin waved me over.

"Thanks for speaking up on my behalf with Ms. Capstone," I said.

"So, did you get a raise? No? Too bad." Kin laughed. "Maybe you stick to turning carrots for a while. Lots to do this week. I won't be here rest of week. I got a small part in the movie."

As I started in on a mountain of carrots I thought that everyone had a part in this movie except me.

On the way home I stopped at a newsstand and asked for a copy of Saturday's *Globe Tribune*. On the bus I searched through the paper for Marius Lippencott's column. I found it on page 5 along with a photo and signature of the columnist. I blinked in surprise when I saw the heading — "Stupor Star."

Only a year ago actor Johnny Random was being hailed as the one most likely to save Hollywood from the mediocre. He had just won an Oscar for his role in *Man From Magalluf*. I've never understood how these awards are selected but movie critics tripped over themselves to jump on the bandwagon and laud this Tinsel Town saviour, describing him as "brilliant," "on a roll," "beyond his own comprehension," and "unstoppable." In short, the best thing since sliced bread.

I find this surprising, since *Man from Magalluf* was, after all, only Random's second film. His first, *Night On the Veranda*, one of the biggest flops ever, was forgotten in the orgy of praise that followed *Man from Magalluf*.

My mother frequently quoted that old adage "One swallow doth not a summer make," and I've always believed it. After what I witnessed last night, I'm convinced that Johnny Random had already had quite a few swallows, and I don't mean the feathered kind. The critics may soon be eating their own reviews. Success seems to have gone to this actor's head, although judging by last night's performance, it wasn't just success.

This "star," who makes about $70,000 a day, was being entertained at taxpayer's expense, along with other actors and crew of Pocket Money Pictures. The mayor and council of Summervale threw a small party to show their appreciation to Pocket Money Pictures for choosing their city as the site for the filming of part of *Funeral at Feng-t'ai*. Shooting begins sometime next week.

Of course, scribes (free loaders), including yours truly, from various news media attended to cover the event, partake of the free food and drink (champagne was provided), and bask in the glitter of some of Tinsel Town's tinsel.

Now I don't claim to be a film critic, but I do know a bad performance when I see one, and believe me, this performance stunk out the house. It would seem that our "star" is so mesmerized by his own aura that he feels all he needs to do is show up and people will applaud.

Admittedly, answering what are sometimes repetitive and often inane questions may be irksome, but hey, when you're tagged with the star logo, it comes with the territory.

If Summervale was a country it could declare Johnny Random *persona non grata*. But it isn't. But does that mean it has to tolerate the type of boorish behaviour witnessed last night?

The reception was being catered by The Ritz, an establishment which prides itself in quality service and good food (I've stayed there often), and indeed The Ritz's catering staff didn't let this fine hotel's reputation down last night. The food and service were magnificent. Dessert was crêpes Suzette flambé on request and our "star," in a fit of pique because he wasn't served his crêpe flambé before some of us lesser mortals (he hadn't asked for one), grabbed a bottle of brandy off the serving cart, slopped it about, and almost managed to flambé himself.

The kid trying to serve him, who probably makes minimum wage in a part-time job, was doing his best. Johnny Random owes that kid, The Ritz, and the people of Summervale an apology.

Fame, for this self-indulgent stupor-star, appears to be a heady experience, although he already had a snootful when he unwittingly almost became an even hotter Hollywood property by self-immolation. If this was not just a random act (sorry, but I can't resist the pun), he may find that fame can be as fleeting as a flash in the pan and can get snuffed out quicker than a crêpe Suzette.

I didn't understand all the words that Marius Lippencott had written but I understood enough to know he was calling Johnny Random a jerk.

I'd just got home when the phone rang. I answered it. It was Celia.

"How did it go today?" she asked.

I told her everything and she sounded pleased. I also told her about Kin getting a part in the movie.

"How come you weren't in school today?" I asked.

"I was in real early to get permission to have most of the rest of the week off. With shooting on the film starting this week, I was asked if I could work overtime. By the way, I found out that I'm not the best boy. I'm just a runner. Calling me best boy was just that creep Ralph's idea of a joke. Hey, Joanne showed up today. She quit her job with outside catering but she wasn't too happy to find that Ralph isn't really with casting, and she had to help me change light bulbs."

"Still," I said, "she gets to work on the set. Maybe I should get friendly with Ralph." I laughed. "Everyone's getting something to do on this film except me."

15

I'D REMEMBERED TO COLLECT my work experience sheet at The Ritz and I turned it in to Mr. Shamberg.

"Oh, Harry. I heard there was a kerfuffle at some reception that The Ritz was catering. Would you know anything about that?"

I wondered, *how much does Mr. Shamberg know?* Probably everything. If my whole class knew yesterday, he must have found out by now. Mr. Constantine, my homeroom teacher, was sure to have mentioned it in the staff lounge. It was in his classroom that all the cartoons of me had appeared on the chalkboard.

"Um. I was there," I said. "It was a reception for Pocket Money Pictures at city hall and Johnny Random, the film star, spilled some brandy when he was being served a flaming crêpe. The brandy caught fire, but no one was hurt," I added hurriedly.

Mr. Shamberg gave a small smile and said, "No mountain bikes involved, I take it. By the way, I got the insurance settlement for mine."

When I got to homeroom class, the previous day's excitement and kidding had almost been forgotten, although David Craven, the class cartoonist, tried to revive it briefly by drawing a waiter with a dragon's body and my head. Flames were shooting out of my mouth and were hitting a plate, piled high with pancakes, in front of a very startled-looking Johnny Random.

At The Ritz it was very busy. Mountains of vegetables were waiting to be turned, but late in the afternoon I was pressed into service with the room service crew. Mostly I just had to set up the carts while Mario and Helga did the ordering and delivered the food. Just before it was time for me to leave, a woman from personnel arrived and told Mario that someone called Lucille, who was supposed to relieve Helga, had telephoned to say she was ill and the hotel couldn't get a replacement.

Mario groaned. "We're really busy and Harry is going home in a few minutes."

"I could stay until nine o'clock," Helga said, "but no longer."

"How about you, Harry?" the woman asked. "Could you stay? It'd be until eleven but we'd pay for a taxi home, and, of course, we'd pay you overtime wages."

"Okay," I said, "but I'll have to phone home."

"Great," the woman from personnel said. "Give this voucher to the cab driver and the hotel will take care of it."

"Oh, what about supper?" I asked.

"You can have supper in the staff cafeteria," Mario said. "You can go now, if you like. It won't get real busy until a little later."

Things had quieted down when I got back and Mario went to have supper. Helga showed me how to put in some of the food orders on the machine that rang up the orders in the kitchen. First, you punched in the time and your name.

Then the food order and room number. Each food item had an abbreviated code and most of the codes were on a list near the phone. New York steak with horseradish sauce was NY/Horserad, w/w meant whole wheat bread, and w/t meant white.

It got busy again for a while and around 9 p.m., Helga went home, leaving Mario and me. Then things started going crazy. Mario was answering the phone every few minutes, punching up orders and barking out orders for me to set up carts.

"I don't know what's going on," Mario said, "but there must be a big party in room 1103. That's the fifth big order in a row. Now they want forty baked potatoes." He rushed off to the kitchen and returned with three orders for that room, and asked me to deliver them while he took care of another call that came in just then.

When I got off the elevator with the cart on the eleventh floor, I could hear the noise down the hallway. The door to 1103 was wide open. I could see it was a fairly large suite but it was jam-packed with people. The noise was almost deafening. Music blared, voices were raised, and there was a lot of laughter. I rapped on the open door a number of times before I was noticed.

"Hey Vincent, it's room service," one of the party-goers yelled across the room.

A short guy with a red face and a drink in his hand pushed his way through the crowd. He swayed a little and spilled some of his drink. When he reached the cart he lifted the lids off the food. "Where's the baked potatoes I ordered?" His voice was slurred.

"They're being baked," I said. "They'll be here soon."

"Okay."

I handed him the bill and a pen to sign for the food. He swayed some more, dropped the pen on the floor, and then got down on his hands and knees to look for it. I found it and held it out to him. He was still kneeling on the floor when he scrawled his signature on the bill and I could leave. I was glad to escape.

When I got back down to room service, Mario was putting the final touches to the baked potato order and was heading off to deliver it.

"Hold the fort, Harry. I'll be back as soon as I can. There's one more order on the go in the kitchen. It's for the fifth floor. If it's ready before I get back, take it up, okay?"

The phone was quiet until the kitchen rang to say the order for room 543 was ready. I went and got it and I was surprised to see it was a plate of fried liver. Mario hadn't returned, so I put it on the cart and took it up. A little grey-haired lady answered the door of room 543 and smiled when I wheeled the cart into her room. A screeching yowl came from the bathroom and I jumped in surprise. The lady put her finger to her lips and whispered, "My children, Sammy and Felicity. It's past their supper time and they don't like to be kept waiting."

I guess I looked puzzled. This lady looked a bit old to have kids, and not too many kids I know eat only liver. And why were they making such weird noises in the bathroom?

As the lady signed the bill, the yowl came again, louder this time. Then I understood. Sammy and Felicity were cats. I wondered how she'd got them into the hotel.

"I never go anywhere without them. Please don't say anything." She winked at me and pressed a five dollar bill into my hand.

"I hope your, um, children enjoy the liver. Thanks." I winked back at her as I closed the door.

When I got back, Mario was looking frenzied. "That party in 1103 is getting wild. They want ten more baked potatoes. And I've got two other orders for other rooms. Andrew is having a hard time keeping up in the kitchen. He's an apprentice, and the only one on. Henry, the other cook, cut himself badly and had to go to the emergency room. He may not be back. Usually things are slowing down by now."

Mario went off once more to 1103 and took another order with him for the seventh floor while I delivered one to the eighth. I got back without incident. There were no wild parties or cats in the room where I made the delivery, but when Mario returned a few minutes later, there was potato in his hair.

He was fuming. "I'm calling security. They were having a food fight. I got pelted and I think they've already wrecked the room."

He dialed a number and explained the situation. "Now, maybe we'll have a little peace." He'd just hung up but the phone rang immediately. He swore under his breath as he picked up the phone and took the order.

"This one is easy. I'll take it. There's only a half hour left until the end of your shift. I go until one, but now that security is sorting things out in 1103, it should be fairly quiet. Just wait until I get back and then you can grab a cab and leave."

I relaxed. Mario collected the order from the kitchen and went to deliver it. I watched the clock on the wall. Only a few minutes left before I could go.

The phone rang. I jumped. I picked it up. "Room service," I said.

"Okay. I want a hot, *now really hot*, roast beef sandwich on whole wheat and fries, sent up to room 2015 right away."

I thought I recognized the voice.

"And I'll have a bottle of Perrier."

I did recognize the voice. It was Johnny Random, and he sounded drunk.

Nervously, I repeated the order.

"Yeah, you got it. And hot, none of this cold stuff. Make sure it's hot."

"Yes, sir." I hung up. I looked at the food list and started punching in the abbreviations as the phone rang again. *Hot R/B w/w wt fri* I punched in, as I picked up the phone. "Hello. Room service."

"Harry, it's Mario. I'm stuck in the elevator. I can't get hold of security. I guess they must still be dealing with the party in 1103. I'll wait a few minutes and try again. Can you manage by yourself?"

"Yeah, okay." I hung up.

The phone rang again.

"Room service," I answered.

"Some service." It was Johnny Random. "Where's that hot roast beef sandwich I ordered?"

"Coming, sir."

"Make it snappy."

I desperately needed Mario back here. I didn't want to be the one to deliver Johnny Random's sandwich. When I hung up, Andrew was on the phone right away to tell me the sandwich was ready.

There was nothing else I could do. I ran to the kitchen and got the food. "You did say hot, hot," Andrew said.

"Yeah, yeah. Mario's stuck in the elevator. He can't get hold of security."

"It's okay," Andrew said. "Relax."

Relax, I thought. It was easy for him to say. He hadn't been the one to almost set Johnny Random on fire the other night.

I nervously rapped on the door of 2015.

"Come in," Johnny Random hollered.

The door was unlocked. I pushed it open and manoeuvred the cart through the door. Johnny Random was sprawled in an armchair watching TV. A half empty bottle of liquor was on a table beside him.

He didn't take his eyes off the TV but waved his arm to indicate I should put the food on the table beside him.

As I was unloading the cart I recognized the soundtrack on the TV. Johnny Random was watching himself in *Man From Magalluf*.

Maybe I can just leave the food and sneak out of here before he notices it's me. But what about the bill? Could I forge his signature? No. I'd pay for it myself if I didn't get it signed. No point in even mentioning the bill. Just leave the food and get the heck out of there.

I had just put the last of the utensils on the table and was about to back out of the room when Johnny Random reached for his glass, took a large swallow, and glanced at me. Then he stared.

"Haven't I seen you somewhere before?" He waved his drink and some of it slopped over the edge of the glass. I noticed his eyebrows looked painted on like Ms. Capstone's.

"I don't think so, sir," I replied shakily. Desperately, I hoped he didn't remember me. Maybe he was too drunk that night, or maybe he was too drunk now. "The bill, sir." I held out the bill and a pen.

"I hope this food is hot." He kept looking at me like he was searching his memory as he signed the bill. He raised one finger, like he was about to remember, when his elbow slipped off the arm of the chair and he slopped a large quantity of his drink onto his pants. He swore. I grabbed the signed bill and fled.

When I got back to room service, Mario was there. "What a night!" he complained. "Hey. It's way past your bedtime. You'd better grab a cab at the front door."

As the cab pulled away from the curb an ambulance cut its siren and pulled up to the front door of the hotel. That party in suite 1103 must have really got out of hand, I thought.

16

I WAS IN SHOCK. A cold shiver ran through me. I stared at the headline in the *Morning Independent* — "Johnny Random Hospitalized."

I could feel my heart beating, fast. What had happened? Would I be blamed again? Then I calmed down a little. He probably just got really drunk or something.

I peered through the plastic front of the newspaper box and tried to read the rest of the article. "Oscar award–winning film star Johnny Random was rushed by ambulance to the hospital last night. Random, who is in the city to star in the movie *Funeral at Feng-t'ai*, was suddenly taken ill. The nature of his illness was …" I couldn't read anymore because the newspaper was folded in the box. I fumbled in my pockets for some change but all I found was the five dollar bill the little old lady with the cats had given me the night before.

I was halfway to school and our newspaper was probably still on the steps outside the house. Dad was working night shift and Aunt Phyllis had left to go to the film set long before I got up. Mom was the only one in the house and she didn't bother with the newspaper. I could run back and get it, but I'd be late for school.

I didn't have anything to do with Johnny Random getting sick, I reasoned. All I did was deliver his sandwich. There was nothing to worry about. Right?

I was wrong.

"Harry, we need to talk." Mr. Shamberg was waiting in the hall, a worried look on his face. I followed him to his office.

"I had a call from a Ms. Capstone at The Ritz early this morning, real early in fact, at six. She didn't sound too happy to say the least. She wants you to go to her office at The Ritz right away. But first, you'd better fill me in. All I know is that the film star Johnny Random, a guest at The Ritz, has been taken to hospital. What happened?"

"Nothing."

"Nothing! That Ms. Capstone didn't think it was nothing. I was still half asleep but I know she chewed my ear off. And she told me what she thinks of our work experience program, which, in her words, will never be allowed to darken the door of The Ritz again. She said she should never have agreed to allow the program into the hotel after what happened last year. I didn't know what she was talking about. I tried to tell her we had nobody from this school at The Ritz last year. She wouldn't listen. She was screaming at me about how can anyone possibly forget the *Ice Sculpture Incident*.

"Then I knew what she was talking about. I'd heard about it from a colleague at Eastridge High. It was one of their students. Apparently, this kid had a bit of a romance with one of the maids at The Ritz and they were fooling around in the freezer. There was a giant ice sculpture in there, which was to be the centrepiece for a big dinner for this delegation from Latin America, including some vice president or other from Paraguay, I think.

"Anyway, the two lovebirds in the freezer managed to knock over the ice sculpture and a couple of large chunks fell off. They tried sticking it back together somehow, but, just after the dinner started, it came crashing down in bits and just about flattened the Latin-American vice president. He thought it was an assassination attempt.

"But why am I telling you all this? That Ms. Capstone tore such a strip off me this morning, she has me all shook up. She wouldn't listen when I tried to explain that it wasn't a student from this school with the ice sculpture, but it was useless. She was really worked up. So what did you do?"

"Delivered a sandwich."

"What kind of sandwich?"

"Roast beef. I only delivered it. Honest. Why? What happened?"

"I was hoping you could tell me," Mr. Shamberg said. "From what Ms. Capstone said, it sounded like Johnny Random is at death's door."

I gasped. "You mean food poisoning? But I didn't cook it. I only took it up to his room."

"You're sure?"

"Of course I'm sure."

"Well, this Ms. Capstone seems to be blaming you for something. I can't repeat some of the language she used. But she was adamant you get to her office right away. You'd better go now. I'll clear things with your other teachers. When you get back, come and see me."

* * *

"Hold all my calls, Cynthia," Ms. Capstone barked at a speakerphone on her desk. She was wearing the same black widow spider dress she'd worn the first time we'd met. She took a deep breath, which made her loom up even larger across the desk as she glared at me, and this time I really felt like her prey.

She let out her breath, which sounded like a menacing hiss, and knitted her brows. I don't mean that in the usual sense of just frowning. She was really knitting, or at least her eyebrows were. They jumped and circled and seemed to cross over each other, and I almost expected to see a small black sweater or sock emerge from the bridge of her nose.

"What … do … you … have … against … Johnny … Random?" Ms. Capstone spoke between gritted teeth and pounded her desk to emphasize each word. Her telephone, daybook, and in and out baskets jumped with each pound. So did I. She stopped pounding but she still gritted her teeth and almost snarled. "First you try to set him on fire and now you try to poison him. What is it with you people today?" I noticed her face matched the bright red of the sash on her dress.

"At The Ritz you don't get second chances. You're fired! Do you understand? Fired!" Her fist crashed once more onto her desk.

I jumped again.

"I wanted to tell you that in person so that there can be absolutely no misunderstanding," she snapped. "Your paycheck will be mailed to you. And I want your identification badge. Now!"

"It's in my locker," I mumbled.

"At school?" Ms. Capstone glared at me.

"No, here. At The Ritz."

"Turn it in before you leave the building," she hissed menacingly.

"But …"

"But what?" she thundered.

"Well ... what happened?"

"What happened?!" Ms. Capstone screamed. "You ordered a hot roast beef sandwich with chili peppers. Nobody in their right mind eats chili peppers in a sandwich. Why did you do it? Did you think it was some great practical joke? Mr. Random is allergic to chili peppers and had a severe allergic reaction. Heaven knows what the lawsuit will cost this hotel."

"But ..." I protested, "I ordered a roast beef sandwich I ..."

"Yes, a *Hot, Hot* roast beef sandwich. I have it right here. Here's the order slip." Ms. Capstone snatched the order slip off her desk, lunged forward and thrust it in front of my face. "You are *H. Flanagan*. That is *your name* on the slip."

I nodded. I could see *Hot Hot* on the slip. I don't know why I'd punched that in twice, and I didn't know what it meant. I couldn't recall all the codes on the wall chart. I could only remember punching in the order and answering the phone at the same time. I did remember Andrew asking me, when I went to the kitchen to pick up the sandwich, if I meant *Hot Hot*, but I didn't know two *Hots* meant chili peppers.

The intercom on Ms. Capstone's desk buzzed.

Ms. Capstone pressed a button and yelled, "Cynthia, I thought I told you to hold all calls."

"Sorry, Ms. Capstone," Cynthia's voice sounded nervous, "but it's Mr. Rudsnicker. I thought you'd want to take his call."

"Very well." Ms. Capstone looked at me. "You may go. Go!" She pointed to the door for emphasis. "And don't forget to turn in your identification badge," she yelled as I retreated.

Ms. Capstone picked up the phone. "Yes, Mr. Rudsnicker. I'm devastated. I've just fired the person responsible."

As I rode the bus back to school, I wondered if I'd have to join Joe Straka in the auto wreckers, or, even worse, work on the assembly line at Luxottica Lighting with Dad in order to finish my credits. Maybe Mr. Shamberg wouldn't be able to get me taken on anywhere, and I'd have to repeat the course next September, which meant I'd finish high school four months after everyone else in my class. It was a real bummer.

I was trying to explain the whole thing to Mr. Shamberg when the phone on his desk rang. He picked it up.

"Shamberg." Mr. Shamberg suddenly tensed. "Yes, Ms. Capstone. Yes, he's right here."

I groaned inwardly. What now? Was I going to be named in Johnny Random's lawsuit? I almost laughed at the thought. Go ahead and sue me. All I had was my bus pass and the five bucks from the cat lady.

"Yes, Ms. Capstone, he'll be there by two. Thanks." Mr. Shamberg hung up. "That was Ms. Capstone, and she didn't take my head off. She said that you must be at The Ritz at two o'clock. I'm not sure why, but she said it was important. Don't do anything to upset her. That lady scares me."

"Me too," I said.

* * *

We were face to face again but Ms. Capstone's face colour had returned to normal and she wasn't yelling. "You are still fired, but Mr. Rudsnicker of Pocket Money Pictures called me on your behalf." Ms. Capstone's eyebrows only flickered. "I told Mr. Rudsnicker that we couldn't take any more chances with you. The hotel's reputation is at risk. Anyway, it's not as if your whole career is ruined or anything, unless, of course, your heart was set on making the hotel industry your career. Is it?"

"Um, no," I mumbled.

"I thought not. We couldn't possibly give you a reference, anyway. Be that as it may, I asked you to come back because Mr. Rudsnicker asked to speak to you. I'll telephone his suite and tell him you are on your way up. I'll have security escort you." She picked up the phone and dialed.

"Mr. Rudsnicker, it's Yolanda Capstone. I have Mr. Flanagan in my office. Shall I send him up? Very well." She punched a button on the phone and dialed again. "John, I'd like you to escort Mr. Harry Flanagan to Mr. Rudsnicker's suite. Mr. Flanagan is in my office. And please wait outside Mr. Rudsnicker's suite to escort Mr. Flanagan off the premises when he leaves. Thanks." She hung up.

"You can wait in the outer office. John will take you to Mr. Rudsnicker."

"Thanks," I mumbled as I hurried out.

I'd only just stepped out of her office when a dark-suited guy with a brass name tag on his lapel that read "John," appeared. "Mr. Flanagan?"

I nodded and followed him.

We rode silently up in the elevator. I stared at the numbers as they flashed above the door and wondered what Robert Rudsnicker would have to say to me after I'd almost done in his star actor.

John nodded to the security guy sitting on the chair on the twentieth floor, and knocked on the door of suite 2014. Robert Rudsnicker opened the door almost immediately and waved me in, just as the phone rang behind him. He went to answer it as John pulled the door closed behind me and left me standing in the hallway of the suite. I couldn't see Robert Rudsnicker but I heard him pick up the phone.

"Rudsnicker. Oh, Colin. Th-thanks for getting back, back to me so fa-fast. Just a min-minute." I heard Robert Rudsnicker take a couple of deep breaths. "There, that's better. Just getting control of my stammer, Colin. Look, you know I talked to your agent. I assume he filled you in on the situation here. Good, good. How soon can you get here? Tonight's flight? Great!

I'll have my driver pick you up at the airport. You'll love the script. The part's made for you and you were always my first choice, but you know that. Great, see you tonight." I heard him put down the phone.

"Harry? Harry, where are you?"

I walked further down the hall to where the suite opened out.

"Ah, there you are. Robert Rudsnicker." He held out his hand and I shook it. "Have-haven't we met before? But of course, I saw you at the reception. Have a seat. Look, I'm sor-sorry about your job. I tried to persuade Yo-Yolanda Capstone to take you ba-back on bu-but I'm afraid there was no-nothing I could do. She was ad-adamant. She's a bit of a bat-battle-axe. Excuse my stammer. It's something I'm try-trying to con-control." He paused and took a few deep breaths. "It's all in the breathing. I couldn't save your job, but I wanted to meet you anyway to see if there was anything I could do for you. You see, I don't know if you realize it or not, but you've done me and Pocket Money Pictures, although they don't realize it yet, a tremendous favour."

"I'm not sure I understand," I said.

"Oh. Well, that was Colin Jang on the phone. You know him, the ac-actor. There I g-go again." He paused and breathed in and out a few times. "Sorry. Well, Colin is flying in tonight to take over the lead in the film I'm directing. I couldn't be happier. You were apparently instrumental in getting rid of Johnny Random, or maybe he got rid of himself. Whatever. He just wasn't working out and there was no way I could break his contract without Pocket Money Pictures paying out a fortune. But then you came along. There was one clause in the contract that gave us an out. If Johnny Random fell ill and couldn't continue on schedule, we were off the hook. I believe his drinking and your sandwich did the trick. He knew he wasn't supposed to mi-mix al-alcohol and pep-peppers."

He paused to breathe again. "This breathing business — it's a trick an old lady actor friend taught me. Anyway, it was Johnny's own fault, so to speak. He might have had a slight reaction to the peppers, but with the booze, he did himself in. He won't recover for at least ten days, and it lets Pocket Money off the hook. They won't have to shell out much to break the contract, and I've been able to get the star I want, Colin Jang. And, we've only just started shooting. It couldn't have worked out better. Is there anything, apart from getting your job back, that I can do for you?"

I hesitated. "Would there be any chance of getting a job in the film as an extra?"

"Is that all? Done. I'll write you a note for Henry Orsini. He's in charge of the extras and getting the battle scenes organized. Oh, you'll have to take a few days off school. Would you like me to call someone there to fix it?"

"Just Mr. Shamberg."

I almost whooped.

I was going to be in the movies!

17

"YOU'RE WHAT?" DAD LOOKED up at the ceiling the way he always does when he wants you to think what he's just heard is totally unbelievable.

"I'm in *Funeral at Feng-t'ai*," I repeated.

"So what happened to the great job you had at The Ritz? Did you quit?"

"Not exactly."

"Fired. I thought so." This time Dad only gave the ceiling a cursory glance. "Did Aunt Phyllis put you up to this?"

"Now George," Mom interjected, "Aunt Phyllis had nothing to do with it."

"Nothing to do with what?" Aunt Phyllis had just come into the kitchen.

"Oh," Mom said. "Harry got a part as an extra in the movie."

"Oh my!" Aunt Phyllis exclaimed. "Another actor in the family!"

"Yeah," Dad said, "just what we need. You know you could have been making good money on the assembly line at Luxottica, and maybe getting a future career for yourself. This movie thing will only be for a few days."

"Oh for heaven's sake, George," Mom said. "Don't start harping on that again. Harry just isn't interested in working at Luxottica. He has other interests. You're just going to have to accept that."

"If I'd known you were interested, Harry," Aunt Phyllis interrupted, "I could have spoken to Robert on your behalf. But what about school?"

"I'm getting the time off as part of the work experience program, and it's only for a few days."

"Yeah, right," Dad mumbled.

"There was a rumour going around the set today that Johnny Random won't be starring in the film anymore, and he's been replaced by Colin Jang. I didn't get a chance to speak to Robert today, but if it's true, he'll be delighted."

"He was," I blurted. I couldn't help myself.

"You spoke to him?" Aunt Phyllis looked startled.

"Um, briefly." Now I wished I'd kept my mouth shut and hadn't said anything about talking to Robert Rudsnicker. I didn't want to explain the real reason for getting fired. Dad would only make it sound really dumb.

"So what got you the part?" Dad asked. "Your hairstyle?"

"No. You might say Robert Rudsnicker just knows how to spot a good actor when he sees one." I grinned and winked at Aunt Phyllis, who grinned back.

"Well, it's your funeral," Dad said.

"No, it's *Funeral at Feng-t'ai*," Aunt Phyllis and I chorused together and laughed.

"Well, whoever funeral it is, it isn't going to get supper ready," Mom said. "Oh, you'd better set your alarm early, Harry, if you're going to have to be at the film set early with Aunt Phyllis. I expect you can get a ride with her."

I noticed a worried look cross Aunt Phyllis's face and I thought I could guess the reason.

* * *

I was up and ready to go by 5 a.m. Aunt Phyllis came rushing up from the basement at the last minute.

"What's the weather like?" she asked.

"I think it's going to be a sunny day."

"Oh good," Aunt Phyllis said. "This will probably be the first day of real shooting. So far it's been only practice. In a way, I'll be glad when it's over. I'm finding these early mornings rather tiring."

When we got to the corner of Aspen Street, where I'd been told I'd be picked up by the Pocket Money Pictures mini-bus, Aunt Phyllis looked a bit uneasy. She looked at her watch. "The limousine is a little late this morning."

I didn't know what to say. I knew Aunt Phyllis didn't get picked up in a limo. Celia had told me she rode the same mini-bus with Aunt Phyllis every morning. Celia got picked up a few blocks away with another group and the bus driver was actually going a few blocks out of the way to pick up Aunt Phyllis. Aunt Phyllis had been late once and the bus had to wait. She'd arrived at the last minute, out of breath, a few other times. Celia said the bus driver was a pretty decent guy and he had offered to pick up Aunt Phyllis outside our house, but it was Aunt Phyllis who'd suggested Aspen Street, a block away.

When I'd phoned Celia's number last night to tell her the good news about being hired as an extra, I'd left it too late and her mom said she'd already gone to bed. It was going to be a real surprise when I boarded the bus.

The mini-bus rounded the corner.

"Oh dear, the limousine must have broken down," Aunt Phyllis said.

I followed her onto the bus and the bus driver greeted her with a cheery smile. "Hi Ms. Papineau. You're bright and early today." Aunt Phyllis gave him a little smile, looked embarrassed, and hurried to find a seat.

"Hello young fella. You Harry?" The driver grinned. "Welcome aboard."

"Thanks."

Celia looked surprised and waved to me from a seat near the back. I was going to go and sit with her when I noticed Aunt Phyllis sitting by herself, staring out the window, and wiping away a tear.

I motioned to Celia I was going to sit with Aunt Phyllis and she smiled back at me.

I sat down as Aunt Phyllis brushed another tear from her lined cheek.

"Oh Harry, I'm just a foolish old lady. You knew all along that I didn't ride in a limousine, and my part in the movie is really tiny. I only pretended I was more important because your father always makes me feel foolish. It's silly, I know, but I do exaggerate. I always have. You must think I'm a compulsive liar. But I do know Robert Rudsnicker. That part is true. He did give me the part, even if it is small." Aunt Phyllis looked crestfallen. "This will be my last acting job. I'll retire after this. I'm just getting too old."

"It's okay, Aunt Phyllis," I said. "I know you know Robert Rudsnicker. He's grateful for what you did to help him with his stammer. He told me so himself."

Aunt Phyllis's face lit up. "He told you that?"

I nodded. "And don't worry about Dad. He doesn't really mean any harm. It's just the way he is. He bugs me too. If you want to let Dad keep on thinking you're picked up in a limo every day, your secret is safe with me. But I don't think he'd really care. He wanted me to work at Luxottica Lighting. It's the only job he's ever had and he's happy there, and he hoped I'd work there too. But what I really want to do is get into acting, like you."

Aunt Phyllis was smiling. "It isn't easy, but it can be a wonderful life."

"I think I'd like to go to acting school if I can get in after I finish at Crestwood."

"Oh, that would be wonderful." Aunt Phyllis beamed. "I'd love to have gone to acting school when I was young but we never had any money. I ran away from home to follow an acting life and my father never forgave me. I have a little money set aside now, and I'd be more than happy to help you after you finish school. It would make me very happy, in fact." She squeezed my hand.

"Thanks, Aunt Phyllis." I gave her a quick peck on the cheek and half expected a few hoots or catcalls from some of the people on the bus, but nobody said anything. If the bus had been filled with Crestwood kids, I'd have really heard about it, but the only one from Crestwood was Celia. I glanced back and smiled at her. Most of the others seemed to be catching up on their sleep.

The bus swung through the gates and coasted down the hill to a large parking lot out of sight of the set, and pulled up beside several other buses. We climbed off and Celia walked with me and Aunt Phyllis.

"Aunt Phyllis, I think you already know Celia, so I don't really need to introduce you, right?"

"We've only just said hello a few times," Celia said, "but I've heard a lot about you, Ms. Papineau, from Harry. He said you've had quite an acting career."

Aunt Phyllis smiled and said, "Oh, I expect Harry was probably exaggerating. It runs in the family, you know." Aunt Phyllis's eyes were twinkling and I was grateful to Celia for saying just the right thing.

"I'm not working at The Ritz anymore." I grinned at Celia. "I got hired as an extra and Mr. Shamberg okayed the whole thing. I'll tell you about it later, but I've got to find Henry Orsini and find out what I'm supposed to do."

"I expect the first thing he'll do is send you to makeup," Aunt Phyllis said. "You don't look very Chinese to me. That's where I'm headed. It's that tent over there. And you'll find Henry Orsini outside that green trailer, giving everyone their orders for the day."

Celia looked pleased. "I'll maybe see you at the lunch break and you can tell me all about how you got the job. Right now I'm off to make sure everything that's supposed to be plugged in, is. Including the coffee pot." Celia waved. "See you later."

I found Henry Orsini where Aunt Phyllis said he would be. He was a tall, broad-shouldered guy with a drooping Mexican-style mustache and he was wearing an Australian bush hat. He was directing a group of Asian-looking guys to the costume tent as I approached.

"Crikey, mate! Who are you?" He gave me a broad grin as I handed him the note Robert Rudsnicker had given me.

He scanned it quickly. "Oh, Harry. Good on ya, mate. I've heard of you. I hear we can thank you for getting us a real actor for this film. It would have been a total flop otherwise. That Johnny Random was a real galah. So you want to be an extra. You don't exactly match the part for a Chinese mob scene. And what happened to your hair? Well, never mind. Makeup can do wonders nowadays. Here. Sign this release form, and this, and you'll get paid."

I quickly signed the forms.

"Ya see that marquee over there." Henry Orsini pointed. "Go in and tell them that Henry wants you to look like a young Chairman Mao." He gave a hearty laugh. "They'll fix you up. Then pick up a costume in that Quonset hut. I want all the extras up behind that hill over there," he turned and pointed, "in a half an hour. Good luck. And as they say over here, have a nice day, mate."

He turned to give instructions to someone else and I hurried to the large makeup tent he had called a marquee. Inside it seemed huge. Bright floodlights hung from a beam that ran along the inside of the peak of the roof, and along one wall a row of mirrors, each one surrounded by light bulbs, faced a row of chairs filled with actors getting made up. It was like a huge barber shop, only much more brightly lit.

"Can I help you?" A young, dark-haired guy in a smock approached me.

"I'm an extra for the mob scene. Henry Orsini wants me to look Chinese."

He grinned. "Henry believes in miracles. But we'll see what we can do. I'm Jack." He showed me to a seat in front of one of the mirrors. The lights surrounding the mirror almost dazzled me.

Jack flung a smock over me and went to a table behind me to get something. I glanced down the length of the tent and was startled to see Aunt Phyllis. I didn't recognize her at first. It was only the green slacks protruding from under her smock that gave her away. I was startled because Aunt Phyllis didn't look like the Aunt Phyllis I knew anymore. She was now an aging dowager, like she'd said. Her hair was a huge jet-black wig done up in a bun, and her face looked decidedly Chinese. But it wasn't just the makeup and wig. She was already into the role of the rich Chinese noblewoman, and she looked so aloof it gave me the impression everybody around her were merely there to attend her. I couldn't believe the transformation. She really looked the part. *There's some hope for me*, I thought.

Jack returned and started smearing brown makeup onto my face and up into where my hairline should have been. Then my jaw dropped open. In the mirror I saw Colin Jang walk behind me. He was about my height and size and was shorter than I'd thought when I'd seen him in the movies.

He grinned at me as he dropped into the chair beside me. "Hi kid. What's your name?"

"Harry. Harry Flanagan," I mumbled. Jack was smearing makeup around the corners of my mouth and I'm sure my words sounded distorted.

"I'm Colin Jang," he said. "Are you part of my peasant mob?"

"Uh, yeah."

"Well, let's make it a good one, Harry," Colin Jang said, then closed his eyes and shut up when a girl started working on his face.

I didn't know what to say, but I didn't have to say anything because Jack said, "Hold still now. Close your eyes and don't talk." He started doing something around my eyes with what felt like a soft, blunt pencil.

The next thing I felt was a wig being jammed onto my head, but before I could open my eyes, Jack said, "Keep your eyes closed please. I just have to add a bit more eyeliner."

I couldn't believe it when he finally allowed me to look at myself. It was unreal. Harry Flanagan had disappeared, and I was staring into the face of a real Chinese guy. The eyes, the skin colour, the jet-black hair — everything was perfect. A final bit of makeup on my hands, forearms, feet, and ankles completed the picture.

"Now try not to touch your face," Jack said. "Costumes will set you up with the rest."

Ten minutes later I was milling around with about five hundred similar-looking extras in a long, rocky gully behind the hill. Like most of the others, I was wearing a pair of ragged, somewhat short, baggy black pants and a pair of primitive-looking sandals. Now I understood the reason for the makeup on my feet and ankles. Quite a few of the crowd were wearing straw conical hats while others wore a kind of sweatband on their heads, or nothing at all. I'd been given a sweatband, which would help to hold on my wig.

I noticed several women in the crowd and a number of what appeared to be older people, and even a few younger kids. This was, of course, going to be a peasant uprising and not an organized army. For weapons we had an assortment of things. A few carried old muskets, a few more had old-looking swords, but most of us had long sticks, or wicked looking farm tools like sickles and forks. I'd been given one of the sticks.

I glanced at the guy beside me and grinned when I recognized Kin. He was dressed in the same kind of outfit that I had, except he was wearing a hat.

"Hello, Kin. You nearly had me fooled. For a minute there I thought you were really Chinese, but you couldn't fool me," I kidded. "I'd know a Vietnamese guy a mile away."

He stared at me for a moment, then his face broke into a grin. "Harry! You look good. Like real human being now. You quit The Ritz?"

"I got fired. I was never going to be very good at it anyway."

"Don't worry, Harry. It was good training for this job. At The Ritz you fight with food, turning carrots, potatoes, melons. Here the only difference is we fight for food. I have to give you a new Chinese name now. Chan Mao. Hairy One." He laughed.

"Okay everybody. Quiet!" Henry Orsini was standing on a huge rock above the gully, bellowing at us through a megaphone. "Now most of you went through this yesterday.

Remember to spread out. You're not a real army so you don't have to march. You've walked a long way already. When you get to the top of the gully, hurry around behind the rocks and get back to the start of the gully as quickly as possible and start over. Remember, we want five hundred to look like two thousand. Where are the bullock carts? I want one of them at the head of the column and one about the middle. The bullock carts can only go through once or twice, so we need a few shots with them."

A cart pulled by a couple of oxen and loaded with small barrels of gunpowder and a small cannon squelched past in the muddy gully. The wheels on the cart squealed like they needed oil as it took its place at the head of the column. I could see another one further back. Colin Jang appeared near the front and I saw a big boom camera loom up at the top of the gully. Robert Rudsnicker appeared on the rock beside Henry Orsini as Henry yelled "Ready!"

Someone ran to the front of the column with a clapper board and I heard the shout, "Action."

My heart beat fast as I took what I hoped would be my first steps towards stardom. My film career had begun.

18

THE COLUMN WOUND ITS way up the gully and through the gap at the top. As soon as we reached the top, we raced around the side of the hill and entered the gully again at the other end. At the entrance, four or five people spaced us or combined us with other groups so that the column didn't look exactly the same as we went through again. Some of those who were wearing the conical hats passed them to those who didn't have one, and a few different-coloured sweatbands were added to bare-headed extras. Twice I ended up with a hat on my head.

We kept on doing the same thing over and over, non-stop. A few times I saw Colin Jang in the crowd, helping an old man or old lady, and once he hoisted a small boy onto his shoulder. He made it look so natural, like he was a true leader helping his people struggle along. One of the ox carts came through again and, when it started bogging down, Colin Jang motioned to some of us nearby to help push. I found myself slipping in the mud, shoulder to shoulder with Colin Jang. I hoped I didn't look too excited, but was brilliantly acting the part of a tired peasant who had slogged on foot over many hills already.

I lost track of the number of times we went through the gully but finally there was a loud shout of "Cut! That's a wrap." Everyone immediately halted and rested against the rocks along the sides. I was sweating, splattered with mud, and breathing hard, and the wig made my head hot.

Henry Orsini appeared on the rock again and yelled through his megaphone. "Thanks everyone. Take a half-hour lunch break."

I followed the crowd down the hillside and we entered another large tent that was filled with tables and benches. The food was served cafeteria-style and there was plenty of it. As I loaded my plate I saw Kin ahead of me in line. I hadn't seen him since the first march through the gully. I followed him to a table and was sitting down when I caught sight of Celia. I waved to her and she glanced in my direction, but she didn't wave back. She came close and I called to her.

She stared, then a wide grin lit up her face. "Is that really you, Harry? You look terrific. I saw you wave but I guess I was still thinking of a bald-headed guy from Crestwood High." She laughed as she sat at the table.

"I guess I didn't look too terrific before, huh?" I said.

Celia was still grinning. "Well, I think you look a lot better with hair. What do you think, Kin?"

"Not only hair." Kin chuckled. "I think he should always look this way. Maybe Harry will have to always wear makeup now too." He gave me a nudge. "Celia likes new Harry better, won't be satisfied with old Harry."

I laughed but I felt myself blushing and I was glad of the makeup. Kin was assuming Celia was my girlfriend, but I hadn't even been out with her on a real date.

"Celia, do you think I should show up in Ms. Havershaw's class like this and tell her I'm Harold Flanagan? She nearly had a bird when I shaved my head."

Celia was drinking some juice and almost choked with laughter.

Kin changed the subject. "Yesterday we walked up that valley eleven times. I counted. Today only six."

"I don't think you'll have to do it again," Celia said. "I heard Henry Orsini and Robert Rudsnicker talking and they seemed happy with what they'd shot. I think you're going to try the storming of the castle next. So are you gonna tell me how you got hired, Harry?"

"Mmn." I was stuffing food into my mouth. I was ravenous. As soon as I swallowed I said, "Maybe I'd better tell you later, tonight on the bus. It's kind of embarrassing."

"Does it have anything to do with Johnny Random ending up in the hospital?" Celia asked, laughing.

I nodded and I felt myself blush again. "It wasn't my fault though, but Ms. Capstone fired me anyway — bad publicity for The Ritz or something."

I didn't have to say anymore just then because Henry Orsini came in and started yelling into his megaphone. "Can I have your attention." As soon as there was quiet, he went on. "Thanks everyone for the job this morning. I think we got what we wanted. After lunch, I'd like you all to assemble out in front of the castle. I'll give you your instructions there. If we get through the castle fight we might have time for a go with the train. You have ten minutes left. Enjoy the rest of your lunch."

"What happens with the train?" I asked.

"It gets hijacked by the rebels," Celia said. "Remember, I told you. It's going to be combined with the mob storming the castle on foot. The train will come over the bridge, filled with rebels firing on the castle, and the mob in the street will join them. I expect they're going to rehearse the bit where they charge on foot first and then to do the train shots later. It all has to be timed right."

"So who gets to ride the train?" I asked.

"Me, I hope." Kin grinned. "Too much walking already."

"I dunno," Celia said. "They'll probably use all of you to storm the castle and then pick a few for the train. I've been setting electrical charges on the bridge all morning. They are supposed to go off when the third coach is rolling over the bridge, to simulate fire from the cannon in the castle. The people in the castle somehow know that the train has been taken over by the rebels."

"It sounds really exciting," I said.

"It's gonna be really noisy, anyway," Celia replied. "I know they are going to use a model of the train for one part because they are going to derail the last car and have it plunge over the bridge. With the real train, they have it set up so the last car simply uncouples and the rest of the train continues into the town.

"The first two cars will be filled with extras, but, because of the explosions and the fact it's a long-distance shot, they have the last car filled with dummies. The dummies all have muskets that fire off blanks. I had to help Ralph set up timing switches to fire the blanks. It's really creepy in the car, because some of the dummies are controlled by computers and can move. Ralph scared the heck out of me yesterday when he made one jerk back, like it had been shot, just when I was putting the timing switch on the musket."

I caught sight of Aunt Phyllis sitting at a table at the far end of the tent. She was looking very regal and haughty, as if it was a real indignation to have to eat with such rabble. I wondered what she had done all morning and what her part would really be like.

"I'd better go," Celia said. "It's quite a hike up to the bridge and I've got to help Ralph and Joanne finish laying some more charges. If I don't leave now there'll be a long lineup at the washroom. See you later."

Celia's mention of the washroom reminded me that I'd better go too. It could spoil a whole film sequence if I was attacking the castle and instead of diving for cover behind a bush in the face of withering fire, I had to stand behind the bush to relieve myself.

19

WE ASSEMBLED ON THE open ground in front of the castle. Henry Orsini climbed up a small stepladder and yelled through his megaphone, "We've decided to shoot the street scene first. It shouldn't take long. I want all the street people to get your props and take up your positions. Those of you not in the street scene, move back and try to keep quiet. Right, get that bullock cart and the rickshaws at opposite ends of the street."

In a few minutes the street was filled with extras playing the parts of ordinary townspeople. Some balanced heavy loads on the ends of thick bamboo poles. A few pushed heavily laden handcarts through the mud. The cart with the oxen and the rickshaws were manoeuvred into position. When all was ready, Robert Rudsnicker took a deep breath and bellowed, "Quiet on the set." The clapper board was held in front of the camera showing the number of the scene and take, and Robert Rudsnicker called, "Action." The street came to life.

Two cameras, mounted on platforms, were at both ends of the street while another, with a whole crew of people on the cart, rolled silently along a track on the outside edge. Robert Rudsnicker and Henry Orsini rode on the cart, watching the action.

As the ox cart moved past the castle, from out of the crowds on the street, seven peasants emerged and moved towards the castle gates. They were yelling, "Rice, food for the people." Outside the castle gates, two uniformed guards tensed and brandished wicked-looking swords as the protesters moved closer.

A rickshaw's progress was momentarily stalled by the protesters as they passed in front of it and then, from up the street, there appeared a small procession. It consisted of a sedan chair, carried by four bare-chested slaves and surrounded by six guards. Between the guards, and beside the window of the sedan chair, walked a grey-bearded old man wearing a long black robe. The protesters caught sight of the sedan chair and converged on it, yelling their protests and waving their fists.

Another rickshaw came on the scene and, for a moment, there was a small traffic jam as the sedan chair, the two rickshaws, and the protesters appeared to merge.

There was some pushing and shoving as the rickshaw pullers and the protesters and the guards came together. One of the guards raised a staff and beat one of the protesters to the muddy ground, blood pouring from a wound to his head. This seemed to make the other protesters more incensed and their yelling increased.

Suddenly the curtains of the sedan chair were pulled back and there sat a grim-faced Aunt Phyllis, or rather, the rich Chinese dowager and mother of the ruler of the province.

"What is the meaning of this outrage?" she screamed at the old man with the beard.

"They are asking for rice. They say they are starving." His voice quavered, as if he was fearful of the woman in the sedan chair.

At the same moment the protesters were tangling with the guards. One of the slaves was jostled and he stumbled and almost fell. The sedan chair leaned suddenly to one side.

Aunt Phyllis screeched, but the slave recovered his footing and the sedan chair was righted. "Unworthy, lazy rabble," Aunt Phyllis screamed at the protesters. "Um. Let them eat cake."

"Cut," yelled Robert Rudsnicker.

The action came to a stand-still.

There were a few snickers in the crowd of extras beside me and I heard Aunt Phyllis say, in an embarrassed voice, "I'm sorry, Robert, I got carried away. I'll get it right next time." At that moment she was no longer the noble Chinese dowager but just Aunt Phyllis. Then I saw her pull herself together and she became a woman with authority over the peasants around her.

"Okay, Ms. Papineau. Okay everybody. Let's take it from the top," Henry Orsini hollered. "Back in position, everyone."

The injured peasant got up out of the mud and someone from makeup sponged off the fake blood and pulled a new headband around his head. It took a few minutes before everyone, including the oxen, were back in position and "Action" was called again.

I held my breath and kept my fingers crossed in the hope that Aunt Phyllis wouldn't blow the line again. This time she got it right, screaming the correct line, "Unworthy, lazy rabble. If they need more rice, let them grow more."

The guards beat the peasants into submission and, with help from more guards who came running from the castle, those that were still standing were dragged away. As the sedan chair disappeared inside the castle gates, Robert Rudsnicker yelled "Cut."

The "dead" peasants came back to life and the street emptied as Henry Orsini climbed onto the stepladder to face us once again.

"Okay, mates. The next sequence will probably take a while so we're going to run through it one more time. We'll be filming, in case we can use some of it, but we'll be doing it again tomorrow. Now, most of you know what to do, but yesterday, when we rehearsed it, some of you didn't fall down when you were hit. Remember, the fire from the castle is mostly from the cannon. When the explosions go off in the open ground, if you are within a few feet of them, you would not be able to keep running. You must fall. The experienced stunt people will take the lead and will activate the explosions by tripwire. Now, we don't want anyone getting hurt. There'll be a lot of dirt flying around and a lot of noise. Grab yourself a couple of earplugs and go to the top of the hill behind you. Those of you with muskets know what to do. If you don't take a hit, keep on running right up to the castle walls. Right. Let's have a go and see how it looks."

We congregated just above the crest of the grassy hill that faced the street and castle. A couple of leading extras got us spread out and lined up in rows. When the signal was given, we were to charge down the hill, across an open space of almost three hundred metres, and try to make it to the castle. Most of the others had practised this already, but I'd no idea when I'd know if I'd been killed or wounded. I remembered when I was a little kid playing cowboys and Indians with Leonard Wooley and Matthew Beagle. We always argued about whether we'd been shot or not when someone yelled "I got you" and our games often fizzled out because no one wanted to fall down and die.

The lead extra raised his hand, waiting for the signal below. His hand dropped and we started running down the hill. I was in the back row. When the leading group reached the flat area, there were loud explosions and spurts of dirt started flying into the air. I was glad of the earplugs we'd been given. The noise was deafening. I saw puffs of smoke coming from the castle walls and the small valley echoed with the *whomp* of the explosions. From a small hillock behind us, the rebel force's one small cannon fired in reply. The ground I was running on seemed to be shaking. Clouds of smoke joined with the flying dirt as we ran.

I ran past a number of "dead" or "dying" rebels and saw others with muskets quickly kneel and fire their ancient weapons. I swerved and almost stumbled when one of the extras unexpectedly knelt in front of me to fire. A huge explosion about thirty feet ahead of me flung dirt into the air and I found myself running right through the middle of a cloud of dust and smoke. I was passing more of the "dead" when, to my left, another explosion flung a severed bleeding arm across my path. I hoped the arm was just a special effect, and Henry Orsini's comment about not wanting anyone to get hurt didn't go beyond a little dirt in the face or eyes. My feet hit the edge of the street and I almost tripped over the railway track.

Ahead of me, some of the remains of our rebel force were clambering up the rough walls, while another group was trying to batter down the gates using a heavy-laden handcart they had seized from someone. A couple of "dead" guards lay on the ground outside the gates.

I followed the closest rebel and raced for the wall. We reached it and started climbing up. My weapon, the long pole I'd been given, made the climb more difficult. I was halfway up when a face appeared at the top of the wall above me and, whoever it was, took a swipe at me with a thick staff. He missed, but I felt the breeze of the staff as it swished past my head. Some of these extras played for real. If I'd been a little higher, I'd be lying at the foot of the wall by now, with a real bleeding head and one heck of a headache. I was about to try going up again when I heard "Cut" being yelled all around. I dropped to the ground, somewhat relieved.

"That was better," Henry Orsini yelled. "We'll have one more go tomorrow and also do some close-ups of hand-to-hand fighting on the walls, but right now we want to try the train scene while the light is still good. Those of you riding in the train scene, get yourselves up there and the rest of you, get well back out of sight."

About fifty of the extras started up the outer edge of the hill. Most of them carried muskets. The rest of us went back towards the foot of the hill we'd just charged down and sat on the grass.

Kin joined me. "Harry. You're still alive." He grinned. "This is the first time they use the train. Interesting to watch."

Robert Rudsnicker and Henry Orsini rode a golf cart up the hill after the extras that had left. We waited quite a while before we heard the puffing and rumble of the train and saw the smoke appear above the hill to our left. The train rounded the side of the hill and started along the short straight stretch towards the bridge. The small black engine was straining to pick up speed and a steady stream of white smoke fussed from its smokestack. Trailing wisps of steam drifted from its undercarriage. The three old-fashioned passenger coaches appeared, filled with rebels who crowded the narrow windows facing us. I knew the last coach only held the dummies, but they looked real from where we were. The train rumbled onto the bridge and, as the front wheels of the third coach reached the bridge, there was a small puff of smoke between the second and third coach. The third coach was uncoupled. The train with the first two coaches pulled ahead, leaving the third coach behind, coasting to a stop on the bridge itself.

The train picked up speed and started down the slight slope into the main street of the town. Musket fire could be heard from the rebels in the coaches and, when the train came parallel to the castle, the brakes were applied. As the train screeched to a halt I noticed a camera crew on a hydraulic crane, filming from inside the castle walls. The rebels were firing on the castle and, on our side of the train, the windows were empty.

Henry Orsini and Robert Rudsnicker arrived back on the golf cart and the action came to a standstill.

We were all called to assemble on the street in front of the castle while Henry Orsini, Robert Rudsnicker, and Colin Jang had a consultation. Colin Jang had been riding in the engine. Then Robert Rudsnicker called it a day after he had Henry Orsini explain to us that tomorrow, when we made the charge down the hill, the train would also come over the bridge and join in the battle for the castle. Colin Jang would lead the train rebels and the rest of us who were still alive would use the train as cover, and slip between and around the coupled coaches to finish the attack on the castle.

* * *

"You like this better than cooking, Harry?" Kin was grinning as we walked to the bus parking lot. My wig and makeup were gone. "Look," Kin said, "your girlfriend. Maybe you should grow your hair back. I think she likes you better that way."

I thought Kin might be right, but I wasn't really sure I could consider Celia my girlfriend yet. I was pleased to see her chatting with Aunt Phyllis by the bus.

"Hi, Harry. How'd it go?" Celia smiled.

"It was pretty exciting and I didn't get killed. At least, no one told me to play dead, so I just kept running."

Aunt Phyllis gave me a wan smile. "I think you'll have to carry on the family tradition if there are going to be any more actors in our family. I'm getting too old, it seems, for this game. I was mortified today when I blew my lines. It's probably time I retired."

"I thought you made a great rich Chinese dowager," I said. "You had me convinced. And you got it right the second time."

"Thank you. Yes, I did get it right the second time. But my memory isn't what it used to be, and yesterday I said something silly too. I think I said rice cakes. Today, 'Let them eat cake,' was even worse. I know my last part was in a play set during the French Revolution, but there's no excuse. I've never had a part with that line before. Imagine mixing up the French Revolution with this era. There's simply no excuse for it."

I sat beside Celia, across the aisle from Aunt Phyllis, and I tried to cheer her up.

"You shouldn't think of quitting, Aunt Phyllis. You really did a great job. So you blew a line. Lots of actors do that, even Colin Jang, I bet. But I don't think Robert Rudsnicker could have found a better actor to play your role. How do you get that high and mighty look, you know, the way you look proud and stuff? That must come from experience."

"Oh. I don't know." There was a twinkle in Aunt Phyllis's eye. "Actually, when I want to look and feel haughty, I just think of your father when he's going on about the latest wrestling match he's watched. That certainly helps."

Celia and I joined Aunt Phyllis's laughter as the bus pulled out of the parking lot.

20

I WOKE UP LONG before my alarm was due to go off. I was too excited about the upcoming action in the movie to sleep. I lay there, trying to figure out a better way to climb the castle wall if I made it that far again. If I survived the charge across the field, I hoped the same extra wouldn't be waiting for me at the top of the wall. That guy believed in realism, and his swipe at me had come too close for comfort. My alarm buzzed and I got up and dressed quickly.

I'd just gulped down a bowl of cereal and some toast and juice when Aunt Phyllis bustled into the kitchen at the last minute.

"I thought they'd finished filming your parts in the movie, Aunt Phyllis, and you'd be able to sleep in today."

"There's still one last scene, where I flee the castle during the attack, that they might shoot today. But even if they don't shoot that piece I still have to be there. If Robert isn't satisfied with the rushes, there could be retakes. I have to be ready, just in case."

"You mean you have to have your makeup on and everything?"

Aunt Phyllis nodded. "If I'm needed Robert won't want to be kept waiting. There's so much noise when the castle is attacked, it has me quite on edge."

"You'll be great, Aunt Phyllis, you'll see."

We caught the bus as before and I sat with Celia. Aunt Phyllis dozed off almost immediately.

"Your aunt is really sweet," Celia said. "But she was really upset yesterday."

"Yeah," I said. "She loves acting but she thinks she's getting too old for it. She hates to mess up and she was embarrassed yesterday."

I was full of questions. I wanted to know how everything worked.

"Why weren't there any explosions on the bridge when the train went over?" I asked. "I thought there was supposed to be fire from the castle. All I saw was the little puff of smoke when the last coach uncoupled."

"There'll be explosions sometime today, but everything has to be timed properly," Celia replied. "I think they want to do the explosions in one take and the timing is so crucial. They are going to rehearse it once more and film it without the explosions and then try it with them. They'll use the model later and edit all the bits together somehow."

"So what triggers the explosions? Does the train trip something on the track?"

"It's only the third coach that's supposed to take the hits. There's a special trip lever under it that sets them off. I'll be busy checking everything with Ralph and Joanne today."

We arrived on the set and Aunt Phyllis woke up. We headed off to the makeup tent and Celia went to do more work on the bridge with Ralph and Joanne.

I was quickly transformed from Chan Yat Mao to Chan Mao, as Kin had called me with my wig on, and I left before Aunt Phyllis was fully transformed into the Chinese dowager. There was no sign of Colin Jang. *Maybe*, I thought, *he's using Johnny Random's trailer as a dressing room now.*

Henry Orsini had us assemble at the edge of the street as before.

"Today, mates, we're first gonna have one run-through with the train. I want you to charge across the open field like you did yesterday and, just before the first of your mob gets to the edge of the street, the train should pull in. Don't watch the train when you're running across the field. Keep your eyes on the castle. Everything is timed, so don't leave before Chris gives you the signal. He'll watch for mine. Again, remember, if you're close enough to one of those explosions, go down.

"Now, when those of you who've survived get here, make sure the train has come to a stop before you cross in front or between the coaches. We don't want anyone run over. I'm gonna divide you into four groups so some of you will cross in front of the engine, some between the engine and the first coach, some between the two coaches, and some behind the train. When you get past the train, you'll make for the castle walls and the gates like you did yesterday, except the survivors on the train, led by Colin, will already be running ahead of you."

Henry Orsini divided us into groups by having us count by fours. I was in a group to go between the coaches if I made it. Henry said they might have to shoot some close-ups later at the actual walls.

"Now those of you who are going to die in the final charge to the walls know who you are," Henry continued. "Don't forget to activate those blood packs like I showed you. Okay, any questions? No? Good. Let's have a go then."

This time I didn't make it to the castle. Halfway across the open field, the extra running just ahead of me tripped a wire and the ground erupted. Dirt and smoke and the extra flew skywards and I staggered over his body as he hit the ground. "Fall down, kid," he yelled. "You're dead too."

I dropped beside him in what I hoped was a convincing death.

"Lie still now, kid." The extra's face was pressed in the dirt a few feet from mine. He looked like a veteran of battles like these and I took his advice.

The noise was deafening and again I was grateful for the earplugs. Ahead of where we lay I sensed the train approaching and felt the ground tremble beneath me. Although I'd have loved to have looked up to watch the action, I didn't want to have Henry Orsini or Robert Rudsnicker blaming me for an expensive retake. I wondered if I'd get to see myself in this film, and hoped they'd use the bit where I made it to the castle walls. Still, I figured, I'll have one more chance today.

Finally there was silence and the extra beside me got to his feet. "Okay kid. You can quit playing dead now. Let's go see if they're handing out any medals."

The train slowly shunted backwards up the slope out of the town, across the bridge and disappeared behind the hill.

"We're gonna shoot the actual hijacking of the train next," Henry bellowed through his megaphone. "I want all the passengers and the rebels. The rest of you can take a break. There's coffee and doughnuts in the marquee. It'll be at least an hour before I need you. It could even be after lunch, so stick around."

I headed for the food tent and had just grabbed a can of pop and a doughnut when I ran into Celia.

"Want to go up and watch the action over the hill?" she asked. "I just have time for a drink. I have to be up at the train to set up the dummies in the last coach after the passengers are taken off."

We followed Colin Jang, Henry Orsini, Robert Rudsnicker, and the extras up the hill. When we got there, the train was at the far end of the track, several hundred yards from the bend and the bridge. The camera crews were all set up and we stood well back to watch. The passenger extras walked down the track and boarded the train while most of the rebels hid in the bushes beside the tracks.

A huge fallen tree straddled the tracks, blocking the line and Colin Jang and two other rebels stood behind it, with muskets pointed at the train.

Someone waved a green flag at the train as Robert Rudsnicker yelled, "Action."

The train started forward, picked up a little speed, and came to a sudden, screeching stop.

"Cut," yelled Robert Rudsnicker. He had a brief conversation with Henry, who nodded in agreement. Then they called the train engineer and Colin Jang over.

We were close enough to hear. Robert Rudsnicker wanted the train engineer to start applying the brakes a bit sooner because the tree would be easily seen from the engine. He also asked Colin Jang to stand on top of the tree trunk.

They tried it twice more before he was satisfied with the action and he yelled, "That's a take." In the scene, the train screeched to a stop in front of the tree. Colin Jang and his two helpers removed the train engineer and fireman, and the rebels boarded the train. The passengers were left standing with their belongings, beside the tracks.

There was another brief shot, in which one of the oxen was used to drag the tree off the tracks, and then the train, driven by Colin Jang and a fellow rebel, chugged a little way down the track.

"Cut," yelled Robert Rudsnicker. "That's a wrap." He gave Henry Orsini a satisfied pat on the back.

"Okay. Lunch," Henry yelled. "We'll do the final train scene right after."

I caught sight of Zulan Maisoneuve standing nearby. She was dressed in costume. She was wearing blue, filmy trousers under a matching blue silk dress that almost reached her ankles. A pair of brown hiking boots on her feet spoiled the effect.

The train reversed up the track and stopped and everyone climbed off. Colin Jang jumped down from the engine and walked over to Zulan Maisoneuve. "Hi Zulan. Boy, it's darn hot in the engine. I'm gonna get this costume off and leave it here until later. I wore my jeans and a t-shirt underneath because it was cool this morning. You don't look exactly dressed for a hike down the hill either, except for the boots." He laughed.

Zulan smiled. "I know. It was silly of me. Costumes will be upset with me if I get any rips in this silk. But I wanted to see some of the action and I thought I'd miss it if I took time to change. They finished shooting my part in the castle. I couldn't walk up in slippers, so I just grabbed my hiking boots. Not very glamorous. I've got my jeans on too. Maybe I should leave this costume up here, too. There were a few thorny bushes that I got snagged on on the way up. Where can we change?"

"I'm gonna dump my outfit in the last coach. Hop on. They're gonna back the train up a bit more."

Colin Jang and Zulan Maisoneuve disappeared into the last passenger coach and immediately the train engineer backed the train down the line.

"Okay, now I've got to go to work," Celia said to me. "You can help me if you like."

There was nothing I'd have liked better.

I caught sight of Ralph and Joanne hurrying down the track and we followed them. Almost everyone else had disappeared.

As we reached the end coach, Colin and Zulan jumped off, dressed in their jeans.

"Okay," Ralph yelled, "let's be quick." He barely glanced at me and just nodded when Celia said, "I've brought a helper," so I knew he hadn't recognized me. Neither did Joanne, who seemed more intent on looking out a window at the disappearing Colin Jang and Zulan Maisoneuve. I heard her sigh as Ralph ushered her to the far end of the coach.

The dummies were lying out of sight on the wooden seats. Celia showed me how to prop them with their muskets pointed out the windows. A wire was hooked onto each musket to activate the simulated musket fire, which Ralph would control somehow.

It didn't take long, and when we'd finished Ralph did a quick check to make sure everything was hooked up properly. "Good," he grunted. "That's it. All set."

Joanne had already disappeared. I was the last to climb off, and before I did, I glanced down the length of the coach. It gave me an eerie feeling, seeing all those figures looking real, but so silent, crouching at the windows with their staring eyes and muskets trained at nothing in particular.

"I brought a picnic lunch," Celia said. "I put it in the third coach under a seat. I didn't know how much time I'd have to eat today. Now I've got lots of time. I've got lots to eat, too. Want to share it instead of going down to the food tent? They won't need you for an hour yet."

"I'd like that."

We climbed onto the third coach again and Celia retrieved the lunch from under a seat.

"Oh, here's Zulan's costume. It's beautiful. Real silk." Celia ran her hands over the filmy material.

She turned to me with a gleam in her eye. "I'm gonna try it on. She's about my height. I've never worn anything silk before. I'll just try it on for a second. There's no one around. I'll change between the seats. You can turn your back." She grabbed the costume and scurried down the aisle and into a seat beside one of the dummies.

I thought she was a bit crazy. I turned my back and I noticed Colin Jang's costume on another seat. I thought, *why not?* I discarded my black outfit and had Colin Jang's grey pants and shirt on in seconds. His headband was the same red as mine, so I didn't bother with that.

"You can turn around now, Harry. Where are you?"

I bobbed up from behind the seat and Celia gasped. Then she laughed. "You scared me for a minute. I thought you were Colin Jang. How do I look?"

Celia did a little turn in the aisle of the coach. I could only stare. She looked beautiful.

"Well?" she asked.

I grinned. "You look great. Just like my favourite concubine."

"Oh you …" she blushed. "I guess we'd better change back and eat lunch. What's that?"

We could hear someone yelling outside and we both stuck our heads out the same window, leaning over one of the crouching dummies.

"It's Johnny Random! Look. What's he doing?"

"That's the train engineer," Celia whispered. "They're arguing about something. I think Johnny Random is drunk."

"I hope he doesn't find me here," I said. "What's he doing here anyway?"

"Whatever he's doing, he's awful mad." Celia sucked in her breath. "Oh my gosh!"

Johnny Random had suddenly taken a swing at the train engineer. He missed, but the driver staggered back and fell down the grassy slope beside the tracks. Johnny Random jumped into the cab of the engine.

"What's he doing?"

We found out right away. The train gave a loud puff and lurched forward.

"We're moving." Celia gasped and looked horrified.

The train quickly picked up speed.

"We'd better get off quick," I yelled.

"Look. Johnny Random jumped off," Celia cried. "There's no one driving this train. It's going too fast. We can't jump off now."

21

I STARTED RUNNING DOWN the coach towards the engine. "Maybe there's a chance I can reach the engine and put on the brakes," I yelled. "Stay here. I'll see if I can stop it before it gets to the end of the street and runs out of track."

"I'm coming too," Celia called after me.

I stopped at the door that led outside to the gap between the coaches. Celia was right on my heels.

I pushed the door open and looked back over my shoulder at Celia. "Stay here. You'll be safe if this coach uncouples on the bridge like it's supposed to." I had to shout because the rumble of the wheels on the track and the noise of the train itself was much louder with the door open.

"I'm not staying here," Celia yelled back. "It's too spooky with these dummies and the explosions on the bridge will make it worse. Maybe I can help."

I looked at Celia's determined face. I knew it was no use

arguing. With one hand I held onto the handle of the open door behind me and stepped gingerly onto the moving steel plates between the coaches. The plates bucked and shuddered under my feet and threatened to throw me onto the tracks as I reached for the door handle of the next coach.

The door didn't move. I thought it must be locked. I tried again, pushing harder, and it opened. It had only been stuck. I stepped forward, turned around, and reached for Celia's hand. At the same moment I realized we had started crossing the bridge. I glanced down to my left and gasped at the sight of the drop into the ravine. I also caught a glimpse of the railway ties flashing past beneath my feet.

"Don't look down," I yelled.

Celia was about to step across when there was a bang and a puff of smoke. The coupling sprung apart.

For a moment we just stared, as the gap between us widened. We were still holding onto each other's hand but we were being stretched apart. Celia let out a cry and jumped. We landed in a heap on the floor, just inside the doorway of the second coach.

We were scrambling to our feet when there was a sudden jolt and both of us were rocked backwards towards the track. At the same moment, we were deafened by a couple of huge explosions under the coach we'd just left. Celia gasped and grabbed for me.

We'd have been safe now, I thought, if we'd only stayed where we were. Then a third huge explosion shuddered under the coach we'd just left and something went awfully wrong. We watched in horror as the coach jumped from the track and bounced along the railway ties behind us. Then, with a screech of twisting metal, the coach veered off, demolishing the wooden rail on the side of the bridge. It got hung up on the edge of the bridge, teetering there for a moment. Then, with a crunch of splintering wood, it slowly toppled into the ravine.

We were both shaken. Celia was white-faced, but she was the first to recover. She pushed hard against me. "Get inside. Quick, before we fall off."

She held tightly to my hand as we ran down the aisle of the second coach. I pulled open the door at the end and I held my breath as again I stepped out onto the moving steel plates.

Celia was still holding my hand as I reached for the next door and pushed. This time the door opened easily. We made it across and raced through the first coach. I could see the train was rounding the turn, just before going down the incline into the town.

I pushed open the last door and saw the small coal tender with a short ladder up the back of it. The ladder was at least three feet away, and between it and where I stood, there was only a very narrow metal plate to stand on, followed by the coupling, which bounced and jumped just above the tracks. If I stood on the plate to reach for the ladder I'd have nothing to hold on to. The gap was too wide.

I stretched out my hand towards the ladder and hung on to the door frame. I couldn't reach.

"Take hold of my hand again," Celia yelled.

I did, and I was just able to get the tips of the fingers of my right hand around one of the rungs of the ladder. I was wobbling badly with the rocking of the small plate beneath my feet and I felt I was being stretched. "I'm gonna have to jump for it," I yelled at Celia. "Let go of my hand when I yell 'now.'"

"Be careful!" Celia shouted back.

I couldn't look at her. All my attention was focused on the ladder. I couldn't afford to slip.

"Now!" I yelled.

I felt Celia release my hand and I stood for a second on the rocking plate. I thought I heard her stifle a scream as I launched myself across the gap.

My left hand closed on another rung of the ladder, but I scraped my shins against the lower rungs. I scrabbled with my feet and got a foothold. I took a deep breath, scrambled up, and sprawled on top of the coal tender. I turned and looked down over my shoulder at Celia, standing in the doorway of the coach. Her face was white and I noticed a large rip in the sleeve of Zulan Maisoneuve's silk dress.

"I can easily climb into the cab from here," I yelled. "I want you to go to the end of the coach and get a door open. If I get the brakes on, we might stop in time, but we could run out of track. You might have to jump. Okay?"

She nodded, blew me a kiss, and disappeared inside the coach.

As I scrambled into the cab of the engine I prayed that neither Celia nor I would have to jump. We were going at a terrific rate and I realized where we were when the pagoda on the temple at the end of the street flashed past.

I frantically scanned the dials and levers in front of me, looking for a brake. Colin Jang was right. It is awful hot in here. I could feel the heat on my face and I was sweating like mad. I noticed there was a fire burning in a small firebox but I guessed it was just to add realism. I knew the engine was run on diesel fuel.

I reached for a lever and pulled down hard. I jumped as a whistle screeched. Wrong lever. I grabbed another, higher up, and yanked on it. There was a screech of metal and I felt the wheels lock beneath the engine. I'd found the brakes.

I could hear and feel the wheels skidding on the tracks beneath me, but we were still going too fast. The throttle! I had to find the throttle. It must be wide open. The brakes alone wouldn't stop us. I found the throttle lever and pushed it back to the closed position. The engine immediately slowed with a jerk and I staggered as the brakes began to work properly. I glanced out the side of the engine cab and saw we had reached the edge of the castle walls. We were slowing down fast, but not quickly enough. I didn't think we'd stop before we ran out of track.

I leaned out of the cab to try to see how far we had to go before the track ended. People were scurrying out of the way and there was a lot of yelling. I glanced back and was pleased to see a door at the far end of the coach behind me swing open. I saw Celia's hand on the door frame. She was ready to jump if she had to, and I thought I'd better get ready to do the same. I was pretty certain we'd run out of track.

We did. But not the way I expected. The engine was almost opposite the castle gates when it suddenly veered left, off the track, and dropped. I was flung violently against the control panel and I bashed my head on something hard. I fell down and when I picked myself up the side of my head was sticky with blood.

I didn't have much time to think about it. The engine was still moving forward. Huge jets of mud were shooting up all around me. The wheels and undercarriage of the train were acting like the bow of a ship cutting through water as they ploughed a trench into the mud of the street.

I felt dizzy as I tried to look out the little window of the cab to see ahead, but it was plastered with mud. I leaned out of the cab as the mud continued to fly, making it almost impossible to see anything. But I saw enough. We were about to hit the closed gates of the castle. It was too late to jump. I hoped Celia had made it.

There was a loud *whomp*, and, although I'd braced myself, I still took another crack on the head. Stuff was flying past the cab and I guessed it was part of the castle. I took cover under the small overhang of the engine's roof. There was one more jolt and again I landed on the floor.

When I picked myself up, the train had stopped. A strong smell of diesel fuel filled the cab. My head throbbed and I shook it to try to clear it, but that only made it hurt. I was still dizzy as I looked out. The engine had punched through the castle gates and had taken part of the wall with it. The first coach was completely inside the walls and the second about halfway in. Both coaches were leaning and skewed sideways like part of a giant letter Z, but somehow they had managed to remain more or less upright.

As I jumped to the ground and landed in ankle deep mud, there was a loud *whoof* and a flash of fire behind me. The engine's firebox had ignited the spilled diesel fuel. I felt a blast of heat as I struggled to move away, but the mud kept trying to suck me back. A breeze sprang up and the flames engulfed the cab and raced along the coal tender to lick the roof of the first coach. I had to get back there and find out if Celia had got out.

I struggled through the mud to the last door of the coach. The coach was tilted towards me and the door still hung open. I dragged myself uphill into the coach and called, "Celia, Celia!"

There was no answer. Maybe she'd jumped before we hit the gates, I thought. Then I heard a moan.

I found her in a crumpled heap between two seats, not far from the door. There was an ugly bruise on her forehead. She wasn't moaning anymore. She was unconscious.

I struggled to pick her up. It wasn't easy, as I was still feeling dizzy and I had trouble keeping my footing on the slanted floor. Black smoke was beginning to pour through the coach, making it hard to breathe. When I got to the door, flames were spreading along the outside of the coach. I jumped out with Celia in my arms and landed in the mud again. I ducked as another small explosion came from the engine and more flames shot along the side of the coach. I had to get Celia away from there.

Smoke and the blood from the wound on my head stung my eyes as I tried to find a gap in the wall. The second coach almost filled the hole in the wall and there was no room to squeeze through. I spotted a big pile of wreckage, which I thought I might be able to use to climb over.

I stumbled, rather than climbed, up the pile of debris and found I was level with the roof of the second coach. I stepped onto it and staggered along it, out of the castle compound.

I'd almost reached the end of the roof, which was tilted towards the street, when I felt I was about to pass out. I was afraid I might drop Celia so I sank to my knees. Somehow I shuffled over to the edge of the roof and let myself drop to the mud below with Celia still in my arms.

I must have passed out then, because the next thing I knew Celia was gone and Henry Orsini was peering down at me. I didn't recognize him — my eyes wouldn't focus — but I recognized his accent.

"Crikey mate! You're a fair dinkum showstopper if ever I saw one!"

22

I BLINKED AT THE bright, fuzzy whiteness. I was staring at a ceiling.

"Oh. You're awake." A short, dark-haired nurse loomed over me. "You woke up once before but you fell asleep again."

I couldn't remember.

"How do you feel?" the nurse asked.

"Thirsty." My throat felt like it was caked with dust. I sat up. My head felt tight. *I'm still wearing my headband and wig*, I thought. I reached up and found a bandage on my head. The nurse handed me a glass of water and I drank greedily.

"How long have I been in the hospital?" I asked.

"Just overnight. For observation. I expect you can go home today or tomorrow." The nurse fluffed up the pillows behind me and smiled. "The doctor will be in to see you shortly. Oh, you had some visitors, but they've gone off to have breakfast. They'll be back soon."

"What time is it?"

The nurse looked at her watch. "Seven-fifteen."

"Where are my clothes? Can I get dressed?"

"Better wait until the doctor sees you. You can ask her. I have to go now. I'll have some breakfast sent in." She left.

I had to find out what happened to Celia. I should have asked that nurse. I was about to jump out of bed to look for my clothes when the doctor came in.

"Hello, Harry. I'm Doctor Webster," she said. "How's the head? Any headaches?"

"No." I felt my head. "It's a bit sore to touch, that's all."

"You took a couple of stitches." Dr. Webster was shining a light into my eyes and seemed in a hurry. "Everything seems fine. But you'll have to take it easy for a day or two. Your own doctor can remove the stitches in about a week."

"Can I get dressed and go home?"

"Better have some breakfast first. See how you feel then. Your mother can check you out, but only if you feel okay." She left the room.

If I feel okay. How could I feel okay? Robert Ruds-nicker, Henry Orsini, and the whole crew at Pocket Money Pictures would want to kill me. I was in the cab of the engine when it wrecked the castle and started the fire. Harry *Flammable* had struck again. My film career had turned out to be even shorter than my career as a chef.

Celia! I had to find out if she was okay. I jumped out of bed to look for my clothes. I was wearing one of those hospital gowns that don't close properly at the back. I looked in the closet. It was empty.

I opened the door and looked down a long hallway and nearly died. Robert Rudsnicker, Henry Orsini, and Colin Jang were coming my way.

I closed the door. I had to get out of there. I looked out the window. Too high. It looked like I was on about the fifth floor.

I couldn't run away, anyway, wearing only this stupid gown with my rear end hanging out the back. I had to hide. The closet? Under the bed? Too late. There was a rap on the door and Henry Orsini stuck his head around the door.

"G'day mate. Good to see you up and about." Colin Jang and Robert Rudsnicker followed him into the room.

I backed up against the bed. "Look," I said. "I'm sorry about the train. I was trying to stop it."

"We know that now." Henry grinned. "But, I must admit, at first we thought you were some kind of saboteur with kangaroos in his paddock. Robert and I were ready to tear you to bits."

"Well." I paused. "I guess the movie set is ruined."

"It co-could have been wo-worse if you hadn't got the br-brakes on," Robert Rudsnicker said.

Colin Jang and Henry Orsini were grinning their heads off, but I couldn't understand why.

"I must admit it, I was a real panic merchant when I saw you climbing over the wall with that sheila in your arms," Henry said. "I could have sworn it was Colin and Zulan."

Sheila? What did he mean, Sheila?

"Her name's Celia, not Sheila," I said. "How is she? Is she okay?"

"Oh, sorry mate. Excuse the Aussie lingo. Sheila's just a name we use for girls down in Oz."

"But is she okay?" I asked anxiously.

"I'm fine. A bit bruised, but otherwise okay." It was Celia, and she had a small bandage on her forehead. She was followed by Mom and Aunt Phyllis. I saw Mom get a worried look on her face when she saw the three men in the room, and I guessed she thought they were doctors.

Celia, Mom, and Aunt Phyllis hugged me in turn and all of them had tears in their eyes. It was a bit embarrassing, made worse because of the dumb gown I was wearing, which seemed to want to keep parting up the back. I made sure nobody got behind me.

Mom's anxiety was relieved when Aunt Phyllis introduced everyone and then she looked anxious again when she realized they were all from Pocket Money Pictures, and maybe I was in trouble.

"I'm really sorry I didn't get the train stopped in time." I didn't know what else to say.

"We-we're not." It was Robert Rudsnicker. "We-we're glad."

I stared at him as Colin Jang burst out laughing.

"We know about Johnny Random." Colin Jang was still grinning.

"I don't understand," I said. "What's so funny?"

"A cup-couple of-of …" Robert Rudsnicker was excited.

"Take a deep breath, Robert," Aunt Phyllis advised.

Robert Rudsnicker nodded, took a breath and began again. "A couple of our camera crews had the presence of mind to capture the whole thing on film. We've spent all night going over the rushes."

I stared.

"With a bit of editing, mate," Henry Orsini interjected, "thanks to you and Celia here, we believe we've got the makings of a real corker. In other words, a very fine movie."

I gulped. A wave of relief swept over me and immediately I was full of questions. "But why did the third coach jump the tracks?"

Robert Rudsnicker took a deep breath and answered. "We believe the train was going much faster than we'd planned and Ralph, our electrician, may have overestimated the amount of explosives. With the extra speed, the three explosions went off almost together and jolted the coach off the tracks and over the bridge. It was lucky you two weren't in it."

I didn't want to think about that.

"And why did the train leave the tracks and hit the castle?"

"That was the switch," Henry said. "We should have taken it out altogether. It was asking for trouble. Even Blind Freddy could have seen that. We believe that no-hoper, Johnny Random, probably tampered with the switch too. Probably came on the set real early in the morning, before anyone else showed up."

My breakfast arrived, and although I was too excited to eat, I was glad of an excuse to get into bed and get my embarrassing gown under cover.

"Well, we'd better push off, mate," Henry said. "We've got lots to do. Clean up the flaming set." He laughed. "We got the fire out. It's not flaming anymore. But we've got to get that editing underway and do a few small retakes while we've still got those extras."

Robert Rudsnicker took a breath again. "We're all very grateful to both of you. Next week, if you're feeling better, you're welcome to come out to the set. If you feel up to it, I think we might even need a double for Colin here. And I think Pocket Money Pictures could come up with a raise. Interested?"

I whooped. "You bet!"

"Oh, another thing," Robert Rudsnicker continued. "What are you doing this summer?"

"Um. Nothing. Why?"

"Because, if we are going to use you as Colin's double, it would be best to have you with us in China." He turned to Celia. "Both of you, if you like."

We both grinned and nodded.

"Ahem." It was Aunt Phyllis. "Robert, wouldn't they need a chaperone? They're quite young, you know."

"Bu-bu-bu …"

"Oh! Breathe, Robert, for heaven's sake!" Aunt Phyllis admonished.

Robert Rudsnicker grinned. "Just kidding. All right. But I'd make you work. There are no free-loaders at Pocket Money Pictures. I suppose I might need a speech therapist, but I think we might find a few more small scenes for a noble Chinese dowager."

Aunt Phyllis beamed.

They left and Aunt Phyllis and Celia waited outside when Mom produced my clothes.

"How's Dad taking all this?" I asked as I changed.

"He was here most of the night. He was very worried about you. When we found out you were going to be okay, I sent him off to work. I know how proud he is of not missing many days at Luxottica. He didn't want to go, but I persuaded him. He said to tell you he loves you." Mom was close to crying again.

"I went home this morning and got you those clean clothes," she went on hurriedly. "That grey outfit you were wearing is filthy and has blood all over it. I think we should throw it away."

"Not on your life." I grinned.

23

THAT NEXT WEEK WAS quite a week. In fact, it's turned out to be quite a year.

First, the press got hold of the story and wrote up some garbled version about Colin Jang's understudy stopping a runaway train. Robert Rudsnicker had the publicity department put out a press release on behalf of Pocket Money Pictures, and toned down the whole thing. He said it was best, at this time, to get the North American section of the film wrapped up as quickly as possible and not give away too much of the plot. I don't think he wanted it known that the train sequence wasn't actually planned.

Pocket Money Pictures didn't make a fuss over what Johnny Random did, and he checked himself into a private clinic to try to cure his drinking problem. The last time I heard of him, he was about ready to make a comeback.

Mr. Shamberg gave me full credits for the work experience

program with The Ritz and Pocket Money Pictures, and I graduated on time.

The trip to China was fantastic. I didn't have to do much except a few simple stand-in shots for Colin Jang, but I learned an awful lot. It was great having Celia along, even if Aunt Phyllis was acting as our chaperone. Robert Rudsnicker was as good as his word and had the script changed a bit to get Aunt Phyllis into a couple more scenes and she really played her part well.

A special public screening of *Funeral at Feng-t'ai* was held in November in Summervale, and we all went to see it. I couldn't believe it myself when I saw it. The editing job was fantastic. I found Kin and me in the march, and even saw myself killed in the attack on the castle. The train plunging over the bridge still scared me though, and Celia could hardly bear to watch. A lot of the dummies tumbled out of the coach when it went over the bridge and ended up in the bottom of the ravine. They looked like real bodies to me.

It wouldn't have fit in the plot, anyway, but I was glad they'd edited out the bit of me and Celia scrambling between the coaches. I knew I wouldn't have looked too brave.

I looked great though, when I stumbled from the engine, all bloodied and muddy, and staggered along the roof of the coach, over the wall, with Celia in my arms. The rest of my followers, thanks to a few retakes and great editing, cheered madly.

They'd filmed a scene with the rebels pouring out of the coaches inside the castle compound, and a sword fight between Colin Jang and Paul Tinyan.

In the changed script, Paul Tinyan, playing the ruler of the province, was preparing to flee with Li Ching. He'd drugged Li Ching to stop her from trying to escape. This bit fit nicely with me carrying an unconscious Celia over the wall.

Dad thought the film was great. He even gave Aunt Phyllis a peck on the cheek when he told her, "You did great," and he sounded like he really meant it. Dad and Aunt Phyllis had called a truce.

After the screening, we were all invited to a special reception at city hall, this time paid for by Pocket Money Pictures. It was really nice to be a guest. It was catered by The Ritz again, and I noticed there were no crêpes flambé on the menu. I was surprised, though, to see Chef Antonio carving the roast himself. When he served me, I grinned at him and he looked at me curiously, but I don't think he recognized me. I'd let my hair grow back.

Dad has finally accepted the fact that I might want to be an actor. Sometimes, when he's not watching wrestling, he's had a few of his pals over to the house to see the special video version of the movie I was given. Mom and I have to grin every time we hear him in the living room calling out, "There's Aunt Phyllis," and "that's my boy!"

Aunt Phyllis kept her promise. With her help, I've enrolled in college in Summervale and I'm taking drama. After that, who knows? Maybe I'll go to New York to acting school. Robert Rudsnicker wants me to keep in touch with him. He said he'd see what he could do for me in the future.

Oh yeah. Celia and I are dating. Really dating. But our biggest date is coming up soon in Hollywood. We've been invited to the Academy Awards. *Funeral at Feng-t'ai* is up for a number of awards. But the one I'm really hoping that the movie wins is Best Stunt. If it wins, Robert Rudsnicker says I can accept it on behalf of Pocket Money Pictures. I've got my acceptance speech all ready, just in case.

Transmigration
by Nicholas Maes
9781459702318
$12.99

Simon Carpenter is a normal 16-year-old living in Vancouver. Or is he normal? Any type of music drives him crazy. When walking by a homeless person, he can see the world through the drunken man's eyes. And when visiting a pet shop he hears a rabbit speaking to him. To solve these mysteries, he takes the rabbit home, only to discover that a foreign "presence" lives inside it. To make matters worse, this "presence" belongs to an army of souls that has plans to supplant the human race.

Who are these creatures? How do they plan to accomplish their goal? How is Simon connected to them? And if they can watch his every step, how can he stop them? These are questions he must answer … quickly. Nothing is what it seems to be and failure will lead to worldwide disaster.

The Greyhound
by John Cooper
9781554888603
$12.99

Fifteen-year-old Danny is a troubled kid, and trouble always seems to follow him. Things are changing just too fast — his family has moved to a new town, his father is battling alcoholism, and Danny has a hair-trigger temper that causes him problems with the teachers and the other kids at his new school. But as they say, everybody can do at least one thing well, and for Danny it's judo. The dojo is the one place where Danny's aggression can find an outlet, even as he tries to make sense of a life that seems way out of control. As he gets ready for an upcoming competition, things just might be on the upswing in Danny's life. It's all thanks to the arrival of a four-legged wonder, a remarkable greyhound named Long Shot that may hold the key to Danny finding both balance in his life and, especially, a greater understanding of his father.

DUNDURN
www.dundurn.com

Visit us at
Dundurn.com
Definingcanada.ca
@dundurnpress
Facebook.com/dundurnpress
Free, downloadable Teacher Resource Guides

teacher resources
www.dundurn.com/teachers